Entangled

formerly known
as Spellbound

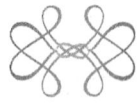

Titles by Jaimey Grant

Connected Regencies:

Honor
Betrayal
Deception
Intrigue
Entangled (Spellbound)
Heartless
Redemption
Forgotten, and other Heartless tales

Short Stories:

My Lady Coward: An Episodic Regency Romance
The 11th Commandment: A Serial Regency in Ten Parts
Gertrude's Grace: A Short Regency ~~Romance~~...uh, Comedy
Assassin's Keeper / Survival in Unlocked: Ten "Key" Tales
Eliza's Epiphany in Whispered Beginnings
The Dragon's Birth (fantasy)

Entangled formerly known as *Spellbound*

A Regency Romance

by

Jaimey Grant

TreasureLine Publishing

Entangled
(formerly known as Spellbound)
A Regency Romance
by Jaimey Grant

E-book edition first published 2008; reissued Jan 2017
Paperback edition first published 2008; reissued Jan 2017
ISBN-13: 978-1-61752-172-0

Cover design by Laura J Miller
www.anauthorsart.com
Stock photos from
www.depositphotos.com
www.hotdamnstock.com
Published by TreasureLine Publishing
www.treasurelinebooks.weebly.com

Entangled
formerly known as Spellbound

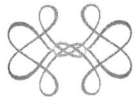

Prologue

January 1820

"It's insane, Raven. He's insane. How can you even consider it?"

Raven Emerson stared at Adam, her slightly raised brows the only sign of her annoyance. Adam's wife, Bri, was strangely silent. Normally, she was full of ideas and opinions, some quite scandalous, but today she was keeping her thoughts to herself. Raven was unsure why this was but decided to spare her friend the necessity of giving her opinion in front of Adam.

"I don't see how my decision is any concern of yours, Adam Prestwich," replied Raven in her throaty voice. Her expression revealed nothing.

"None of my concern?" Disbelief was writ plain on the baronet's handsome face. "And how, madam, do you suppose that?"

His tone had taken on a dangerous silkiness that Raven knew meant he was more than a little perturbed. She didn't care. She was no longer his to command and she'd be damned if she'd let him try.

"I'm not your responsibility now," she told him. "You have a wife and children to worry about. Leave me be."

Adam stared at her. "You may not be my mistress anymore but you're still my friend and my wife's as well." He paused but Raven said nothing. "You cannot have thought this through!" he finally exploded.

"I assure you, I have," she told him quietly—and completely without truth. She caught the look of surprise on Bri's face but ignored it. "Lord Windhaven assures me I will be well paid and have nothing to fear from his family provided I play my part well." A ghost of a smile crossed her lips. "And there is little fear of that considering I've been an actress for years."

"But you have acted in nothing for nearly a year, Raven," Adam pointed out mockingly. "Are you sure you remember how?"

Raven glared at him in response. She was used to Adam's callousness. She had been under his protection for years before he met and married Lady Brianna Derring, a titled lady in her own right and running from her family. Adam's hands had been full to overflowing with Bri's problems and while Raven had been of some considerable help to the couple, she had also been in the way.

Adam released an exasperated breath. "The man must be completely balmy to ask you to impersonate a peeress, Raven. Either that or he views you as expendable. Do you realize they will hang you if you're discovered? And his family will probably be the first to lead you to the scaffold. Can he protect you then?"

Raven shrugged with seeming nonchalance. "He's a duke," she said carelessly. Inside she was frightened but she'd never reveal that to the odious man before her.

A shiver of excitement coursed through her. Her life had become a trifle boring of late—a circumstance she blamed entirely on her past decisions and her belief that she had a penance to pay for giving in to temptation—once with Adam and once with…

She pushed her other indiscretion determinedly from her mind.

While her thoughts were wandering, Sir Adam Prestwich had rounded on her. "You will die, Raven, duke or not. They will not hesitate to kill an actress grown too puffed up in her own consequence. You know the aristocracy prides itself in keeping out the mushrooms and counter-jumpers. It doesn't matter that you were once the toast of Drury Lane, you'll die."

"Adam, please," protested his wife from her perch on the window seat. The actress had become slightly pale during Adam's diatribe.

Adam's severe expression settled on Bri's pleading face. "Am I being too blunt, my love? Should I sugarcoat it and pretend the situation is not as serious as it seems? And what good, may I ask, will that do?"

Bri scowled at him. "Nothing, I suppose, but this is Raven's decision, you know."

"And what is your opinion, madam wife?" he asked, but Bri clamped her mouth shut and refused to answer. "Very well, my lady, don't tell me. But be assured I will hold you personally responsible if I find out you encouraged her in this madness."

Bri offered a feline grin. Adam just shook his head and looked back at Raven. "If you insist on this folly, despite my better judgment, I promise to help in any way I can when you are found out. Which won't be much, all things considered." With a mocking bow, Adam stormed from the room, leaving the ladies alone.

"What do you think?" Raven inquired casually. She studied her friend's face closely and felt an odd sense of relief at the smile lurking just below the surface of Bri's arresting countenance. Then Bri frowned, effectively killing any sense of relief and starting a twinge of doubt in Raven's decision.

"Have you thought this through?"

"Of course I have. What sort of bufflehead do you think I am?"

Bri's left eyebrow quirked slightly. "Honestly, you're attics to let for entertaining acceptance for more than a second. But," her lovely face split into a grin, "I would be a liar if I told you I was not the least bit intrigued. And Lord Windhaven is very handsome. One must wonder why he should have to purchase a bride. Even a pretend one." Her emerald green eyes twinkled wickedly.

Raven smiled back. "Don't let Adam hear you say that. He'd likely call the duke out for daring to be handsome enough to catch your eye."

Bri laughed at that. Raven frowned slightly. "I have only one problem."

"Linnet."

"Yes. His grace doesn't know about her and I can hardly foist an unknown girl on him when I am supposed to be Dunston's long-lost daughter. I highly doubt she would turn up with another young woman in tow."

"I agree. You can leave her here. I know Callie would love to have her friend. And Adam adores your sister."

"Thank you. I admit I would feel more comfortable if she is here."

"I have to know, Raven, what will you do if someone hears of your *reappearance* and chooses to investigate?"

"Lord Windhaven assured me that his family has not left his primary estate for years and the only one that might actually recognize me would be his brother who has not even visited the estate in five or six years."

"I can't say I really care for those odds, Raven."

"Nor do I. But," she said, searching her mind for something to say, "there was something in his expression that struck me as...desperate. I don't know quite how to explain it."

"And you long for adventure," murmured Bri shrewdly.

Raven smiled. "Don't we all." Her smile disappeared. "There is a mystery there somewhere, Bri. And I mean to find out why a handsome and wealthy duke feels the need to trick his family into believing he is engaged to marry."

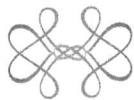

Chapter One

A plain carriage arrived in Mayfair one mild winter day about a week after Raven's introduction to the Duke of Windhaven. It stopped before one of the more modest homes and picked up a young woman dressed in a plain black cloak and drab bonnet. A few boxes and trunks were loaded into the boot and then the carriage pulled away and disappeared.

Some who knew said it was that actress that left. She had caused a minor sensation when she had moved into the respectable neighborhood of Mayfair. Many wanted her gone. They simply assumed their prayers had been answered. They cared not where the carriage was taking her as long as she was gone.

Raven sat inside the plain but well-sprung carriage and let her mind wander at will. Linnet had been sad to be parted from her beloved older sister but her excitement at living with her very good friend, young Callie Prestwich, was a balm. Raven could be glad for it.

Adam's farewell had carried a phenomenal amount of disapproval. Raven shrugged at her thoughts, determined to ignore the uneasy feeling Adam's displeasure caused her. It wasn't that she felt she had to please him. Even with Adam's innate cynicism, he was usually at least partially correct in his feelings.

Bri had withheld her true feelings on the matter and emanated an air of vague indifference that Raven was sure did not fool Adam in the least. She just hoped he would not be too hard on her.

The journey into Kent was not particularly long and Raven soon found herself at what would be her home for the next few months, provided her masquerade lasted that long. First, the carriage passed through the village of Lower Kempworth, near Tunbridge Wells.

Raven stared out the window, being careful to stay out of view of anyone happening to pass by. The village was small, consisting of only a mercantile that served as post office, haberdasher's, linen draper's, and general store, a livery stable for anyone desirous of hiring a mediocre hack or boarding their own hack, and a small inn that had only three rooms available for passersby and visitors. Raven doubted the livery even had a post chaise for rent, it was so small.

Raven was surprised when her conveyance stopped before a tiny cottage on the outskirts of the town. She was about to raise the trap and ask the coachman what he was about when the door was flung open and a pretty girl of about eighteen climbed in. She sat down on the seat opposite Raven and smiled brightly.

"My name is Meg, milady. His grace hired me to act as your maid since you've not yet hired one."

Raven said nothing and just stared at the bubbly girl. She had not thought of such a thing and was secretly surprised that the duke had. It was something she should have realized. The fact that she hadn't made Raven wonder if she was making the biggest mistake of her life to date.

"Don't talk much?" asked Meg. "That's alright. I can talk enough for the both of us, I reckon."

Raven had no doubt of this. "Do you know who I am, then?"

"His grace told me, milady, that he did. He said as how I was to make sure you was taken care of proper like and not made to feel uncomfortable."

"Did he?"

"Oh, yes, milady. His grace is ever so kind and con-consid-considerate!" she finished triumphantly.

"Indeed?"

"Oh, yes, milady. Everyone says so. Even old Mrs.

Barkley down the lane says there is no gentleman kinder than the Duke of Windhaven and she hates everyone."

Raven's black brows rose slightly at this bit of insight. Her only knowledge of the man came from her one interview with him and he had been so mysterious, she had not really known what to think. Anything this effervescent girl might tell her would be welcome.

"And what about his grace's family? I have not yet met them, you know, and I'd like to know a little bit about them before I do."

Meg scrunched up her face for a moment, a look of what one might call distaste crossing her features. "There's his grace's sister, Lady Freya. She's a bit of a wild one and always out and about on her horse. They do say she is touched in the upper works and prone to fits. But she's very beautiful and all the gentlemen admire her, they do.

"Then there's his grace's maiden aunts. Lady Hetty is kind and gentle but a wee bit scatter-witted most times. She was his grace's mama's sister and was every bit as pretty as her grace at one time but did never *take*. The other aunt is Lady Trudy. She is the dowager duchess's half-sister and a good bit younger than her grace. Dr. Campbell says she is a professional invalid," the young girl confided in a whisper.

"His grace's other aunt is the Marchioness of Montgomery and a tartar for sure. They do say she harped her own sons until they decided to have naught to do with her so now she harps at his grace and his lordship to marry." Meg gave a little squeak at this point, as she was talking to his grace's fiancée, and apologized for her impertinence.

"It is nothing, Meg. Pray forget it. Tell me about Lord Windhaven's grandmother."

Meg smiled and obliged her new mistress. "Lady Windhaven is...well, she is..." The maid's eyes grew bigger. "I don't know, milady. Lady Windhaven is a duchess."

Raven knew what this meant. Lady Windhaven would prove to be high-in-the-instep, autocratic, possibly even vindictive. Her word would be law, her preferences everyone's, her annoyances shared. She would make sure Raven was indeed Lady Rachael Elizabeth Eliot, the long-lost daughter of the Marquess of Dunston.

For the first time, Raven realized what a truly monumental task she'd set for herself.

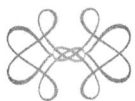

Raven's heart misgave her when she first encountered the Dowager Duchess of Windhaven. The woman was tall, gray-haired, and as haughty as she could have ever imagined. And Raven very much feared the woman knew she was an impostor.

After a brief few minutes in which to refresh herself, a helpful footman—who gave her a sympathetic smile—led Raven to the drawing room. She beheld rich furnishings, expensive paintings and tapestries, and the haughty stares of her new employer's family. The duke was conspicuously absent. Raven filed this fact away for later.

"Lady Rachael, how delightful to meet you," the oldest lady said regally from her throne-like chair at the far end of the immense drawing room, sounding anything but delighted.

Raven curtsied low, but not too low. A younger woman sat on her right, her face pinched as if she were in pain. On the left of the dowager was a woman of indeterminate years who affected the style of a débutante and had a vacant expression on her face. A pug sat in her lap with the same vacant expression on his little smushed face. Raven marveled at how alike they were in appearance.

The woman with the pinched look deigned to acknowledge the newcomer with a regal nod of her head. Raven supposed she must be the dowager's daughter, Lady Montgomery; there was an unmistakable resemblance.

As the vacant lady greeted her absently, a redheaded termagant burst into the room. She stopped when she caught sight of Raven, turned to look at the dowager, and then gave Raven a look filled with such loathing that the former actress was quite taken aback. The girl curtsied mockingly and smiled.

Raven thought the young woman's smile was far more threatening than her earlier look. But she forced herself to smile back. "You must be Lady Freya. I am pleased to meet you." She curtsied slightly and held out a hand. Lady Freya looked down at Raven's hand as if it were a particularly loathsome insect. The duke walked in then and approached Raven. He glared at his sister long enough to cause that young lady to flush and accept Raven's handshake. Then she flounced away to sit by her Aunt Hetty, Lady Mehetabel Hatridge, the late duchess's sister.

Lord Windhaven bowed formally over Raven's hand, apologized for not having appeared sooner, and placed her hand on his arm. He led her over to his grandmother and aunts, performing the introductions gracefully and with the utmost formality. Raven stood stoically throughout, curtsying and nodding as was proper, smiling despite the obvious suspicion and unfriendliness with which she was regarded by all.

Dinner seemed to crawl by although the duke kept up a seemingly endless debate with his grandmother about the current bills presented in Parliament. Raven wondered how he managed to be so up-to-date when everyone knew he rarely left his estate. Newspapers were notoriously inaccurate.

She spoke only when spoken to, using this opportunity to read her companions. She found Windhaven's sister to be rude and quite often offensively so, but she sensed in her an unhappiness that she found truly perplexing. His grandmother was firmly set in her beliefs and opinions, rarely allowing even the duke to override her. The flighty aunt rarely spoke, unless to her pug, Horatio, and then it was to comment on the various persons present at the table as if they were not even there. The other aunt glared at Raven from time to time but otherwise kept her thoughts to herself.

One aunt was missing from their family gathering and Raven had been told she was very ill. When she asked the duke about this and offered to help nurse her, he had gravely informed her that his dear aunt was a hypochondriac and needed nothing more than to have her bottles and powders taken away for a time to prove it. Apparently, Meg had been right in her confidential assessment.

The duke himself was such a grave, solemn man that Raven wondered why. He had not had a very difficult life that she could tell but he seemed to exude a certain disapproval of everyone and everything around him.

Raven looked over at him curiously, careful not to let any of her interest show. He was regarding her with an expression almost of anger and she wondered why. She did a mental check of her appearance. She wore her hair up as fashion said she must, unusual for her, as she preferred to leave the heavy tresses down. Her gown of pale blue complemented her dark locks and made her dark skin seem golden in the candlelight. She wore long gloves, wrinkled just so, and a tasteful necklace of sapphires set in gold. Her brow furrowed slightly at his look.

He looked away, gazing pointedly at his grandmother. "I believe Lady Rachael is looking decidedly peaked after her journey, grandmother, and I would like a word with her before she retires."

Raven sent him a questioning look, which he resolutely ignored, while the dowager rose to signal that dinner was over. The rest of the ladies rose as one and left Raven alone with her "fiancé."

Windhaven signaled the dismissal of all the servants with an imperious wave of his hand. The footmen filed out, followed closely by the butler. In moments, they were alone.

"What the devil are you about?" he demanded.

Raven was stunned but she didn't show it. Instead, she replied mildly, "What do you mean, your grace?"

"I hired you—"

Raven interrupted before he said too much. "Is it wise, your grace, to discuss this here? The walls do have ears, you know." she remarked blandly.

The duke stared at her in disbelief.

Raven sighed. "Your grace, I realize that what I am about to propose is against all rules of propriety but I feel it may be best. If you would like to discuss anything of a personal nature with me, I request that we do so in the privacy of one of our rooms. Since you and I know the truth of our situation…" she let the words trail off, knowing he would grasp that she could not truly be compromised since she was nothing more than an actress.

He seemed to mull this over, his natural inclination to have his own way warring with the wisdom of her request. "Very well," he finally said. He rose to his feet and dropped his voice to a conspiratorial whisper. "I will come to you in ten minutes." He walked from the room with all the confidence of his position in life and Raven felt an unaccustomed pang of envy.

He must have been crazy. Did he actually hire an actress to play the part of a missing woman? Lord, what was he thinking to allow this to even continue?

These and similar thoughts ran through Lord Windhaven's mind as he traversed the halls to the apartment allotted to Raven. He paused outside her door, his hand poised to knock. He took a deep breath and scratched at the hard wood.

The door opened soundlessly. Raven stared up at him, her seductively beautiful face set in lines of expectation but nothing else. She stood silently aside as he entered and closed the door.

Now that he was in her presence, and enough time had passed to cool his anger, Windhaven was unsure how to start. He had thought he had been reasonably angry earlier, but now, he wondered.

"Please sit, Lord Windhaven, and tell me what I did at

dinner this evening that so displeased you," Raven said in her pleasant, throaty voice.

He noticed she was still dressed in her evening gown of blue silk, the fabric swirling around her, showing glimpses of lush curves. He found himself wondering what she looked like naked and was almost relieved at the return of his earlier anger.

"I would like to know, madam," he began, declining the offer to sit, "exactly what you think you are doing here?"

Her dark, perfectly shaped brows quirked ever so slightly at his sharply spoken inquiry. "I was under the impression that you hired me to play the part of Lady Rachael, Lord Windhaven. Am I mistaken in this? If so, I will return to London first thing."

"That is not what I meant. I realize I hired you to play the part of Lady Rachael. What I want to know is, why are you acting like a damned saint?"

Any shred of animation or emotion on Raven's face disappeared. She stared up at the duke and said, "If my acting does not meet your requirements, my lord, I beg that you inform me how I am to act instead of leaving me so completely in the dark. I have agreed to this without prior knowledge of your real reason behind it. What is it you truly wish to accomplish with this masquerade?"

Windhaven's brow furrowed. He began pacing about the room like a lion, his tawny locks winking in the firelight.

Raven sighed, drawing his attention. "Why did you hire

me, Lord Windhaven?"

He stopped moving. He stood as still as a statue, in fact. "I don't know. I thought that if I had a fiancée, grandmother would stop haranguing me about getting married."

"That is highly unlikely until you actually do marry, my lord," she replied logically. She moved across the room with the fluid grace for which she was known and sat in a handsome chair by the crackling fire. "After all, engagements are broken all the time. It would be very easy for you to retain your independence and your grandmother did not strike me as a stupid woman. She would not be satisfied until you were safely wed."

The duke strode over and sat down in the opposite chair. He looked at his companion, not really caring for her unwavering calm. He supposed she was right. The dowager had a way of not giving up until the very final moment. She would hound him until he walked down the aisle with some pretty young thing who would breed him strong sons.

As the duke stared at Raven, an idea began forming in his mind. She had all the behaviors and mannerisms of a lady, so why not? He supposed he could do much worse and Raven was definitely easy on the eyes. In fact, she was a treat to look upon with her glossy black hair, fathomless black eyes, tall, lusciously curved figure, and seductive voice. He felt himself react physically to her charms just thinking about it.

So, the Duke of Windhaven smiled charmingly and said,

"That is easily solved. Marry me."

Raven's famous calm finally deserted her. She had only been in residence less than a day and already the man was determined to toy with her. She felt indignation rising but forced it down and managed to come across as merely annoyed rather than furious.

"I will pretend you did not say that and ask you politely to leave me, your grace," she replied. "If you would like me to continue this charade of being your betrothed, I will oblige you. But please do not play games with me."

"What games?" he asked crossly. "I am in earnest, madam, and in considerable shock that you would not take me seriously."

"Please, Lord Windhaven. If you are in earnest, then you will, like the gentleman you are, allow me time to consider your offer."

The duke rose to his feet and bowed stiffly. She watched him leave the room and wondered why the thought of marriage to such a man—a man who would try to dupe his entire family by hiring an actress to play the part of his affianced bride—had the power to make her heart skip a beat with longing.

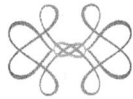

Chapter Two

Raven awoke the next morning with the duke's offer on her mind. She splashed cold water on her face in the hope it would help her see reason as she thought about it some more. She dressed hurriedly in a warm dress of dark wool with long sleeves and a high neck. Then she twisted her long black hair into a knot on her head. All the while, she pondered his offer.

Was she actually considering it? She couldn't possibly! He couldn't possibly! It was true that some members of the aristocracy had actually led their mistresses from the theater to the altar but never a duke and never without having any knowledge of the actress, whether carnal or intellectual.

She flushed suddenly, her poise all but deserting her. She was considering it. The thought of never having to worry over Linnet's future was strong and only for her sister would she dare even think of marrying the Duke of Windhaven.

Splashing water on her face one more time, Raven left her room, completely forgetting that she actually had a maid now. She met her on the stairs. In Meg's hands was a tray bearing chocolate and toast.

"Oh, milady!" exclaimed Meg in distress. "I'm that late, am I?"

"No, Meg," replied Raven reassuringly. "I am a distressingly early riser." She smiled pleasantly. "I have no need of you this morning so if you would like to do something of your own choosing, please feel free."

Meg bobbed a curtsy. "Thank you kindly, milady." Her smile broke forth suddenly. "I think I will go outside. They do say belowstairs that the lake is finally froze over."

Raven waved her on her way and continued down the corridor. As she passed what she discovered was a small bookroom of sorts, the door opened and Windhaven stepped out. She gave a start, her hand flying to her breast.

His pale brows quirked a bit. "Overdoing it a bit, aren't you?" he asked dryly.

Raven frowned. "Overdoing what, exactly, your grace? You startled me, if truth be known."

"What do you know of truth?" he asked sharply.

She lowered her voice dramatically. "I could ask you the same thing, Lord Windhaven."

"Could you? Are you impugning my honor by calling me a liar?"

Raven heard the note of actual anger in his deep voice. "Is that not what you are doing by having me here, my lord? I do not impugn your honor. I made a simple observation."

Windhaven stared down at her. "Why do you behave around me as though you are not afraid of me?" he asked suddenly.

"Because I'm not," she said candidly, too surprised to utter less than the truth. "You are gruff because you find it a pleasure to intimidate people but you are not truly dangerous."

His green eyes darkened considerably and Raven wondered momentarily if perhaps she'd made a miscalculation in her assessment. At that particular moment, he appeared very dangerous indeed.

He smiled suddenly, blindingly. Raven was stunned by that smile. He really ought to do it more often, she thought in wonder. He had a dimple in his left cheek. It was amazing how a smile could so transform a person. He went from being a surly, gruff man to being the hero of every young girl's dreams.

"Lady Rachael?"

Raven snapped back to reality. The duke was looking at

her in concern and she realized it had been he who had called her Rachael. She wondered if she would ever get used to that name. *If you accept his offer, you will have to,* taunted a little voice in her head. *You'd be living a lie for the rest of your life.*

Raven shook it off and smiled. "I'm sorry. I wasn't attending."

"That was obvious," he said dryly. "I asked if you'd step into my office with me. I want to talk to you away from prying ears."

As she preceded him into the rather cluttered room, she remarked, "We do tend to speak unwisely, do we not?"

He grunted in reply, returning to his seat behind a beautifully carved mahogany desk. Raven studied the meticulous carvings intently, impressed with the quality and detail presented. The whole desk was a veritable work of art.

"Do you like it?" the duke asked suddenly.

"Yes, very much," she replied at once. "It is quite the most beautiful thing I have ever seen."

"Yes, I agree," Windhaven said softly. But he was not looking at the desk. He was looking at Raven and she felt her cheeks grow warm under his silent regard. Adam and Levi had never made her feel this way. Windhaven made her feel…loved? That was not possible.

"Well," she said briskly, trying to distract herself from

dangerous thoughts, "what was it you wanted to speak about?"

The duke cleared his throat. "I wanted to discuss what happened last night."

She gave him an inquiring look. This is when he would tell her that he was drunk or jesting, or had made a colossal mistake in asking to marry her.

"Have you given my offer any thought?"

She blinked. "I admit I did," she answered slowly, "but not very seriously since I felt you may regret the impulse later."

He smiled, just a slight twisting of his finely molded lips. "'...Rich gifts wax poor when givers prove unkind.' And all that rot," he told her.

She nodded, amused. "Something like that, your grace."

"I was in earnest then as I am now. If you still think you should not, do not answer me until you know me better." He smiled again but it lacked the whimsy of his earlier grin.

Raven returned his smile. "Very well, my lord. If you insist."

They fell silent, both wondering what to say or do next. Raven found herself pulling slightly at her long sleeve and stopped. She had never been prone to nervousness before and she didn't mean to start now.

Windhaven cleared his throat, looking far more uncomfortable than she felt. "So," he said, thinking quickly, "are you enjoying your visit so far?"

"Yes, my lord, very much," she replied instantly, relieved to have something neutral to talk about. "Although I have not been here very long, I find everything very... intriguing."

The duke thought it was an interesting word to use but forbore commenting on it. "Do you think we can progress beyond the formalities?" he asked instead. She looked surprised at his request and he wondered why. They were supposed to be engaged, after all.

"If you wish," she conceded easily enough.

Windhaven watched the actress as she fiddled with her sleeve again, an action that interested him. Apparently, she was nervous in his presence, a circumstance that surprised him. When he had approached her about taking on this masquerade, she had been calm, composed, and completely in control of her actions and expressions. Now, she seemed as skittish as a new colt. Several times he had caught a look of surprise mingled with unease cross her beautiful features.

"What is your name?" she asked then.

The duke watched a faint blush tinge her high cheekbones and found himself inordinately fascinated by her. He had to admit that it was this more than his annoying family that had prompted his invitation to Windhaven. Who wouldn't be completely enthralled by her beauty and her air of confidence?

Feeling foolish for his moonstruck thoughts, he stood

and turned away from her. "My given name is Tristan," he told her gruffly. "Freya calls me Tris. Grandmother calls me Windhaven." He heard a tinge of sarcasm in his voice and nearly winced. The last thing he needed was to reveal his feelings to a stranger.

"Tristan," Raven said with a nod of satisfaction. "It suits you, I think. Far better than Windhaven."

But Tristan wasn't listening. The sound of his name on her perfect lips made him want to kiss her. And he didn't want to stop there.

Why not make her your mistress? nagged a voice in his head. She had had protectors before. Sir Adam Prestwich had not exactly kept his association with her secret and the Earl of Greville had practically announced it in the London Gazette when he had managed to win her favors.

Tristan shook the thought away. When he had asked her to employ her famed acting skills to help him out, he had promised himself that he would not make physical advances to her.

"While you are here, Rachael," he placed the faintest stress on Rachael, "you should visit my library. I think there is a section there that would interest you greatly."

Her interest piqued, Raven suggested they go there now. The duke smiled. "Very well. Let me finish this and I will escort you."

As he bent his head over the papers scattered over his desk, Raven studied him. His dark blond hair curled all over his head with apparent abandon. His cravat was tied in a perfect example of the oriental and she caught a glimpse of his brightly colored waistcoat through the folds of his severe black jacket.

"Dear God, what is that?" Raven blurted before she could stop herself. She winced at her blunder.

Tristan looked up at Raven, followed her line of sight to his waistcoat and scowled. "It is a waistcoat, my lady," he responded stiffly. His family gave him enough trouble over his choice of odd waistcoats. He didn't need his *employee* doing the same.

"I realize that, Tristan, and I apologize for my exclamation. But what is it?"

Tristan studied her face for signs of mockery. He detected none and so he said, "It is a species of lizard common to America."

"What is it called?" she asked with genuine interest.

"A blue-spotted salamander."

"We have salamanders here in England but not like that," she remarked, a smile of wonder resting on her full lips. "It's beautiful, I think."

"Thank you," Tristan said slowly, suspicious that she was toadying to him.

Raven gave him an exasperated look tinged with amusement. "I am not pandering to your title, oh noble duke. I truly think your sense of style is unique and therefore, pleasing."

"Unique equals pleasing?" he inquired mildly.

"Why not?" she replied with a shrug. "I have often found those with the self-confidence to set their own standards in dress and grooming are very pleasant to be around. Take Lord Petersham for example. He fell in love with Mrs. Brown and wore nothing but brown as a tribute to her. Even his horses and carriage were brown. And he was and still is an amusing man."

"And his addiction to snuff is legendary," remarked Tristan cynically. He himself had no liking for the stuff.

Raven shrugged. "Perhaps. But he went about it just as uniquely as every other aspect in his life. Imagine having a different kind of snuff for every day of the year and a different snuffbox for each as well."

"I'd rather not," responded Tristan dryly. "I don't care for snuff."

Raven fell silent, allowing the duke to finish signing the papers that required his immediate attention. After a few minutes, he set his pen aside and looked up. "Shall we adjourn to the library?"

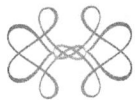

Chapter Three

Raven followed the duke to the bottom floor of the Manor. He took her to the very back of the house and stopped before a set of carved oak doors.

Looking down at her, he smiled. "Ready?"

She nodded, curious at his air of suppressed excitement. He dramatically threw open the doors and Raven wondered if he'd ever considered going on stage. The man would make Kean look like an amateur.

Tristan stepped back, allowing her to enter first. Raven stood on the threshold, amazed at the sight that greeted her.

The library was as big as a ballroom but narrow like a gallery. It took up two stories, with shelves running from floor to ceiling. A balcony with wrought iron banisters was placed at the level of the first floor and ran along both sides of the large chamber. The far end was floor to ceiling windows, hung with heavy burgundy drapes that kept out the harmful rays of the sun during the peak of the day. They were open at the moment, allowing the early morning rays to shine through the stained glass, scattering prisms of rainbow across the room.

Down the center of the room were several tables for study, surrounded by chairs. Some of them had books lying on them, open, as if someone had just left. At the far end, beneath the window, was another table piled high with books and ledgers. A man sat at this table, looking through a book and jotting notes in an open ledger.

As if sensing their presence, the man looked up. "Your g-grace," he said, clearly startled. He stood quickly and crossed the magnificent chamber to meet them. "I d-did not know you'd be in t-today."

"I was not going to be except Rachael desired to see my collection."

Raven offered a friendly smile. "It is a beautiful room," she remarked.

"Indeed, it i-is," agreed the young man.

"My love, this is my clerk, Mr. Harold Muffton. Muff, this is my fiancée, Lady Rachael Eliot."

Raven's heart rate increased at the casual endearment, something that had never occurred before.

"D-dunston's lost d-daughter?" asked Mr. Muffton in

surprise, showing his superior knowledge of Debrett's Peerage. "I was n-not aware you had been f-found." His tone was suspicious.

"I think I allow you too much license if you feel comfortable enough to make that impertinent observation to a guest of mine," the duke said casually. His look was anything but casual, however, and the clerk flushed slightly.

He bowed to Raven. "I beg your p-pardon if I s-seemed...d-disbelieving just n-now," he stuttered apologetically. "I am v-very interested in that p-particular family and I had no p-prior knowledge of your...e-existence."

"It's quite all right, Mr. Muffton," she responded quickly. "I am still a little disbelieving myself."

"Give us a moment, will you, Muff," requested the duke. "I'd like to show Rae around without someone peering over our shoulders." The way Tristan called her Rae caused a tremulous skitter in her breast.

She reflected that the duke was a trifle callous in regard to the clerk but the little man seemed to see nothing unusual in his treatment. He bowed and departed the room, closing the double doors silently after him.

"Now, tell me what you really think," demanded Tristan. His pale green eyes were alight with excitement. She could hardly believe the transformation.

"Like I said, it is very beautiful."

He dismissed her opinion with a wave of his elegant

hand. "Beautiful does not do it justice, Rae, and you know it."

"You are right, of course, your grace," she said seriously, a laugh in her voice and dark eyes. "It is magnificent, stunning, breathtaking, gorgeous, brilliant, picturesque, artistic—" She paused, her eyes twinkling. "Pulchritudinous?"

He laughed. "Very good. I'm impressed," he said when he could.

"Intense, rich, deep, poetic, symphonic, harmonious, prismatic," she said facetiously.

He laughed harder.

"Unequal to anything created by God or man," she added for good measure.

"Stop, please," he begged, his voice shaking with laughter. "I deserved that since I only asked to satisfy my own vanity."

Raven sobered suddenly. "Whyever would you need to do that?" she asked in wonder, studying his handsome face.

He stopped laughing, a closed expression taking over. "Let me show you my prize collection."

Raven wanted very badly to pursue the topic but she wisely refrained from badgering him about it. So she smiled and followed him to the wrought iron stairs that stood to the right side of the doors they'd entered. A matching set stood on the left side, leading to the balcony on that side of the room.

Tristan walked along the balcony to the farthest end of the room. Once there, he reached for a book, pulling it away from the shelf upon which it sat. A catch released and Raven heard the whir of a clockwork mechanism. Part of the shelving moved away to reveal a secret room.

The duke smiled, the look of boyish excitement returning to his face. "Come on," he urged, practically dragging her into the room.

Now, Raven was an actress, and very much a product of her environment. She had read extensively in her quest to be the best in her field and had a great store of knowledge about villains, Gothic happenings, and secret rooms. She held back slightly, a vision of her dead body being found decades later jumping into her mind's eye.

Tristan stopped, glaring down at her. "Whatever is the matter?" he asked curtly.

A look of uncertainty hovered in his eyes and it was this that made her see what a goose she was being. She smiled. "I am sorry. I was overcome with a case of nerves," she told him.

One pale brow quirked. "Indeed? Does this happen often?"

"Not often."

"Considering your calling, that is good," he remarked with a small grin.

"A little fright on stage is good," Raven told him, entering the small chamber. She looked around with interest.

"How so?" he asked, sitting down on the edge of the table that dominated the floor. He set to work lighting a branch of candles since the one window let in very little light.

Raven stared at that window and wondered where it was at from the outside. She determined she would go out one day just to find out.

"If one is nervous, one will not fall victim to over-confidence," she said in reply to his query. She moved over to the window, drawing back the drapes slightly. It was little more than an arrow slit like the ones found in medieval castles. It looked down on the lake that Meg had mentioned just that morning.

"Do you ice-skate here?" she asked suddenly, turning to look at the duke.

She surprised a look of fear in his pale eyes. Her eyes widened slightly at his expression but it quickly disappeared and she was convinced it had been a trick of the light.

"Not very often. Some of the servants will go on their free days." He shrugged. "Freya's been known to go sometimes."

Raven studied his feigned air of indifference and made a mental note to ponder this latest mysterious aspect of his personality later. Glancing around, she noted all the books in this room were very old and appeared to be old playbooks.

She gave him a questioning look. "Do I detect a fan of the stage in you, my lord?"

"You do, Rae, you do," he admitted. "Much as I am ashamed to admit it, I have long wanted to tread the boards."

"Indeed? I can perhaps make that dream come true, you know."

A thoughtful expression came into his eyes. "I am tempted, my dear, I really am." He released a resigned sigh. "It would not answer, however. I have far too many responsibilities here to just abandon them to my brother. He is too involved with his own pleasures to take up the reins of the duchy."

Raven noticed the hint of anger underlying his careless words and wondered at it. She ignored it for the moment, becoming a trifle annoyed by all the mysteries this enigmatic man represented.

"You seem to have every play Shakespeare ever wrote," she remarked, effectively changing the subject. "Which is your favorite?"

Tristan's green eyes rested on her face, his expression carefully blank. "Romeo and Juliet," he replied without hesitation.

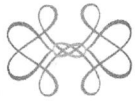

Raven wondered how he managed to make her feel

flustered and unsure of herself with a mere look, and an innocent one at that.

But was his reply so very innocent? Anyone who was anyone knew of her epic performance as Juliet. It was said in every newspaper that no one could portray new love and tragic separation better than she could. And every time the Theatre Royal decided to show the bard's best-known tragedy, there was never an empty seat in the house.

The Duke of Windhaven, although practically a recluse, would have knowledge of this. Especially as he was such a fan of the stage. He would have kept careful account of her activities, as well as those of her fellow actors and those famous before her time. She wondered if he was playing with her by saying Romeo and Juliet was his favorite. Her eyes narrowed a fraction.

Fascinated by the play of emotion on her normally expressionless face, Tristan saw the instant she thought he lied. For what purpose, he could only imagine.

"Rae, I can tell you don't believe me," he said softly. "But I assure you, even before I saw your performance, Romeo and Juliet was ever the best in my mind."

Her face relaxed into its normal easygoing lines. She turned about, offering him a good view of her back, and scanned the shelves that lined the walls. Having found something that interested her, she strode forward and gently removed a newer playbook that was nevertheless worn through use.

"The Marriage of Figaro," she read. "I love this play. And this is an original playbook?"

Tristan rose to his feet and stood next to and a little behind her, looking over her shoulder. "Open it," he commanded gently. She obeyed silently, opening to a random page. He pointed to one page, indicating notes written along the edge. "Beaumarchais's hand. This is from the very first time it was performed in Paris. See, it's in French."

Raven smiled and returned it to the shelf. She selected another book from another section and stared down at it. A shiver raced down her spine. It was a very, very old copy of Macbeth, a play that had always given her an uneasy feeling. She had actually played Lady Macbeth once and secretly hated it. That feeling must have come through in her performance since the play only lasted for a week with her in it. After that, her understudy, a promising girl of ruthless character and rather harsh features, played the role and successfully made her mark in the world of theater.

The book was replaced and she selected another. This time it was a fairly recent edition of Othello. She smiled up at the duke, who stood watching her impassively. "I have always wanted to play Desdemona but I never did have the opportunity. I guess it's too late now."

"We could perform it here, for the family, if you want," he suggested.

"Is that wise?" she replied. "What if someone realizes I

am more of an actress than a lady?"

"You, my dear, are more of a lady than you think," he said blandly. Then he shrugged carelessly. "If you'd rather not, it doesn't matter to me. I merely put it out there as a suggestion. It is winter after all and a little entertainment would not come amiss, I think."

She could see his reasoning on this. "I'll think about it, Tristan."

"You know, I rather like it when you call me that," he commented suddenly. He stared at her face until she lowered her eyes, blushing like a schoolgirl.

She could think of no reply to this that wouldn't sound completely ridiculous and so she remained silent. He seemed to take pity on her, however.

"Come, I have something else to show you." He walked over to a shelf lined with research books about well-known playwrights. Moving aside a huge tome, he released yet another spring catch. This time, the back of the shelf where the large book had sat slid up. Tristan stuck his hand into the dark recess beyond and pulled something out. Silently, he handed his prize to Raven.

She stared it in disbelief. "Another copy of Othello?" She met his intense gaze. "Is this from the first folio?" Her voice sounded breathless, excited, completely unlike herself.

"Actually, no."

"Oh. I know someone who has seen a copy of the first

quarto edition. He said the stage directions were more detailed in that copy. This has the appearance of the folio edition."

Tristan frowned. Her mention of another man annoyed him. "That is a second quarto edition. It was printed from the folio."

"That explains the likenesses," she murmured thoughtfully, missing his look and tone of annoyance. She handed it back to him, being careful to handle it delicately. He returned it to the secret compartment without a word.

"Your home is full of secrets, isn't it?" she said conversationally.

"You have no idea," he remarked dryly.

Raven walked away, allowing him to reset the catch in the wall. Striding around the small room, she gazed at the shelves, looking for something to distract her. Seeing something of interest, she reached up for it but it was on the top shelf, just beyond her reach—which was quite a distance as she was well over five and a half feet tall.

"Allow me," Tristan said from behind her. He stretched his hand toward the playbook she wanted, retrieved it and placed it in her hand.

"Thank you," she said. She opened the book. The title seemed to jump out at her. Romeo and Juliet. How had she known?

Her hand trembled slightly as she leafed through the worn book. She dare not look up at her silent companion for fear her look would reveal how shaken she was.

She was about to become even more shaken. Tristan plucked the book from her hands, saying casually, "You have this suitably memorized, I think." He opened it to a random page, reading the lines in the glow provided by the candles on the table. Then, setting it aside, he took her hand in a gentle clasp that threatened to undo her carefully cultivated composure.

"'If I profane with my unworthiest hand,'" he quoted in a tone that made her breath catch in her throat, "This holy shrine, the gentle fine is this: / My lips, two blushing pilgrims, ready stand / To smooth that rough touch with a tender kiss.'" He suited action to words, bringing her hand to his lips, his eyes never leaving hers.

"'Good pilgrim, you do wrong your hand too much,'"— the words seemed to tumble breathlessly from her mouth of their own accord—"'Which mannerly devotion shows in this; / For saints have hands that pilgrims' hands do touch, / And palm to palm is holy palmers' kiss.'"

Drawing her closer, he continued, "'Have not saints lips, and holy palmers too?'"

"'Ay, pilgrim, lips that they must use in prayer,'" she whispered, transfixed by his steady gaze.

"'O, then, dear saint, let lips do what hands do; / They pray, grant thou, lest faith turn to despair.'"

"'Saints do not move, though grant for prayers' sake.'"

"'Then move not, while my prayer's effect I take,'" he

whispered, drawing her closer still. She now stood within the circle of his arms. "'Thus from my lips, by yours, my sin is purged.'"

Mesmerized, Raven watched his lips draw closer and closer. Her eyes drifted shut as she waited for the touch of his firm lips.

It never came. Her eyes snapped open. She looked up into pale green eyes that held an expression she couldn't name. She opened her mouth to speak.

"Tris? Are you up there?"

Raven's mouth snapped shut. She stared at Tristan, a look of question in her eyes. Tristan's face was taut with annoyance that they had been interrupted. Raven wondered it he felt the same disappointment that she did.

Tristan cleared his throat and called, "One moment." Then he turned his back on her, returning the playbook to its proper shelf. She supposed he would put out the candles next but she didn't wait around to find out.

She walked out of the room and saw the person looking for Tristan. Standing below the balcony was a very handsome young gentleman whose resemblance to the duke proclaimed him to be a member of the family. As she looked closer at the familiar brown curls and pleasant features, she felt a sudden fear clutch at her heart.

Tristan stepped out beside her and gazed down at his brother. "Hello, Grey. When did you get in?" he asked. Raven sensed more than saw the tinge of reserve in the duke's manner towards his younger sibling.

Lord Greyden Cramshaw stared up at the pair above him. His eyes met Raven's and he smiled in that way gentleman did when they thought they had caught a prize. "Well, hello, brother," he said finally, glancing at the duke. "Who is your friend?"

Chapter Four

Tristan didn't care for his brother's attitude. He seemed to think Raven was some available female, ready to jump at any man's bidding. And Grey had a habit of seducing everything in skirts, whether she was a lady or a tart.

A glance at the woman in question showed the duke that something was wrong. Raven was very still, like a marble statue. In fact, with her beauty, she could have been exactly that at that moment.

He nudged her gently. "Anything wrong, my lady?" he asked.

She smiled up at him. "Of course not, my lord. Why would you think anything was wrong?"

"You seem to have turned to stone at the mere sight of

my brother. Usually," he said dryly, "ladies melt when he deigns to look upon them with any sort of favor."

Her black, delicately arched brows rose haughtily at this and Tristan thought in that moment that she really could be Dunston's lost daughter. She was the right age; her features and skin tone matched those of his family. She had a regal bearing that came naturally; it was not something that could be learned. She even had the haughty attitude.

"I assure you, Lord Windhaven, I do not melt at the sight of just any man," he realized Raven was saying.

Her words were a warning and he took them as such. Although, he very much wanted to test that theory at least to the extent of himself.

Favoring her with one of his rare smiles, he offered his arm, saying, "Allow me to escort you to breakfast, my lady."

Raven gave him a confused look. "Breakfast, Tristan? Is it not past that time yet?"

Consulting a watch that hung from a chain attached to his waistcoat, the duke nodded thoughtfully. "Too true," he murmured. "I am, however, lord of this manor and a duke to boot. If you would still like breakfast, I am sure I can make that happen."

"No, please, do not trouble the servants, my lord duke, I can manage with something light, I think."

Tristan gave her a haughty look. "They are servants, Rae. They are here to serve. If they do not, they grow useless and must be let go. I am sure you do not want that."

Raven opened her mouth to tell him a thing or two about misusing servants, but snapped it shut, determined to maintain a civil silence throughout the rest of the morning.

"Rachael Eliot, you cannot possibly think I mistreat my servants," the duke said, again showing an uncanny ability to read her mind. "I think I will choose to be deeply offended by that belief. And to regain my good opinion, you must pay a forfeit."

"What forfeit?" she asked suspiciously.

"You must agree to marry me," he whispered, leaning closer. Then, quite before she knew what he was about, he pressed his lips to hers in a fleeting kiss that was over before it began.

"My dear?"

He was holding out his arm expectantly, and Raven took it mechanically, too shaken by his unexpected kiss to do otherwise. He gave her an odd look, which she returned blankly.

"If this is how you act every time I kiss you, perhaps I never shall again," he remarked with a half-smile and quirked eyebrow.

"Oh, no," blurted Raven, surprising them both. "I mean...well, you do not...oh, dear." She blushed furiously and placed one hand to her brow. "I can't seem to think straight. Perhaps I am sickening for something." It was totally unlike her to be so moved by a mere kiss, especially one lacking in passion, desire, or any feeling whatsoever.

A gleam entered Tristan's green eyes but Raven was so preoccupied with her odd reaction to him that she saw it too late. He clipped her around the waist, pressing her full-length against him, and covered her mouth with his in a kiss that had all the passion, desire, and feeling she could have asked for. His other hand cradled her face as his kiss deepened into something more personal, more intimate than anything she'd ever experienced before. She felt tears come to her eyes and was helpless to stop them from spilling down her cheeks.

"Well, isn't this an interesting sight," inquired a lazy voice tinged with malicious amusement.

Tristan drew away slowly, but there was an angry glint in his eyes that Raven caught. She wondered briefly if he was angry with her but saw almost instantly that it was his brother for whom he held the animosity. She had her back to the other gentleman and so could not see his answering stare of hatred.

The duke looked down at her, saw her tears, and swore softly. Then, louder, "If you want to live to see tomorrow, Grey, you will leave now and await me in the study."

"And miss all the fun?" he queried silkily. "I think not."

Raven could hear him approaching and cringed at the thought of coming face to face with Lord Greyden Cramshaw again after all these years. He had been a persistent admirer of hers when she'd first started acting and had offered her whatever she could have wanted in exchange for her favors. But something had always held her back from accepting the handsome young man. She had sensed something wasn't quite right with him, something possibly dangerous. And now, here she was about to face him again and pretending to be someone else and someone of the peerage at that. If he should threaten to turn her over to a magistrate, what could she possibly do to save herself?

"I will kill you, Grey," the duke bit out carefully. Raven looked up into his eyes and shivered. She believed him.

Evidently, Grey did too. He stopped advancing on them and said, "Very well, Tris. I will leave if you want. But I recommend taking her to your bed. It is rather uncomfortable to make love in this mausoleum." He turned and walked away from them.

Raven tightened her hand on Tristan's arm, as he would have lunged at his brother for that crude comment. He looked down at her in annoyance. "Let me kill him, Rae. I promise I'll clean up the mess."

"If you are serious, I am leaving this instant," she returned, drying her tears with the handkerchief he handed to her. "But since I am sure you could never do such a hateful, mean, horrid, immoral, illegal thing, I will pretend I am amused and stay."

"Why did you cry?" he asked abruptly, effectively changing the subject.

"I don't know," she said, only half-truthful. "Perhaps I

really am sickening for something."

"That doesn't do much for my *amore propre*, you know," he remarked dryly. "I apologize if I frightened or offended you, with either the kiss or the scene with my brother. It was not my intention, believe me."

"And what, sir, was your intention when you kissed me?"

"Merely to prove to myself that I could," he said, his face and eyes devoid of expression. "And isn't it the right of every man to kiss a beautiful woman? And you, my dear Rae, are the most beautiful woman in existence."

"Looks are fleeting," she replied philosophically, "and too much value placed on them leads to heartache and misery. I would prefer to be ugly, my lord, with a squint and hunched-back and loved solely for my mind and spirit and heart, believe me."

"What would you say if I told you I already love your mind and your spirit and your heart? And now I would like to love your form and appearance?" he asked. His face was intent and lacked all signs of jocularity or even the slightest amusement.

"If you are asking me to become your mistress," she answered, trying to control her disappointment and anger, "I thank you for the honor but I cannot accept. I am done with selling my body just to satisfy my lust."

These words made his brows arch in shock, she noticed with a certain amount of satisfaction. Ladies were not supposed to have feelings of lust, that emotion common only to the lower orders and members of the demimonde, of which she was part. She knew this was not actually true. She had enough friends among the upper reaches of society to know there was not an ounce of truth in the belief, not to mention plain common sense would tell one that women were women no matter what social station they possessed. Any serious thoughts he may have harbored about her being in actuality the missing Lady Rachael Eliot should be firmly nipped in the bud now.

He seemed very thoughtful but not necessarily disappointed. She supposed he could be as other men of her acquaintance. Adam and Levi knew there was no truth to the myth about a lady's passion. Tristan wasn't exactly an idiot. She realized any hopes she may have had about his losing interest in her were for naught. If anything, she'd increased them.

Before he could act on what he was obviously thinking, Raven spun around and practically ran from the library.

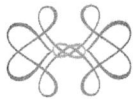

That did not go well, he thought as he followed Raven out at a more sedate pace. What was it about the woman that practically made him lose his head every time she was in the room? It made no sense to him.

He did think she was probably the most beautiful woman in existence; she was most definitely the most beautiful woman he'd ever seen. But even that didn't account for his unpardonable behavior.

Tristan moved through the vast corridors of Windhaven and soon arrived at the part of the house in which resided his study. He didn't want to deal with Greyden now but he knew he had no choice. The man was becoming quite a nuisance, making the family name a byword in Society.

The duke entered the somewhat small chamber and saw his brother rifling through one of the drawers in his desk.

"May I help you?" he inquired icily.

Greyden slammed the drawer shut and gave his older sibling a mocking grin. "You could leave so I could continue searching," he suggested facetiously.

"What the devil are you searching for?"

Greyden shrugged, his grin firmly in place. "Nothing of any import, brother."

"Indeed," murmured Tristan thoughtfully. "Would you mind very much vacating my chair, then?" His tone held that hint of command that he knew his brother detested.

Greyden's grin faltered, a look of malevolence passing briefly through his golden eyes. His look became mocking again, however, as he rose to his feet. "By all means, brother." He gestured to the empty chair. "Please, sit," he invited with false sincerity.

"Grey, if you were not my brother, I'd beat you where you stand and throw you out the window." He frowned. "You are not everyone's brother. Why has it not happened yet?"

"Stow it, Tris," snapped the younger man rudely. His grin returned easily enough, making Tristan frown heavily. "You know, brother," mocked Greyden as he came around the wide desk to stand on the same side as the duke, "I could tell Grandmother who your little friend is. She always did like me better, you know. She would love to have a reason to send you away."

Tristan gave his brother a confused look. "To what are you referring?"

Greyden's smile became genuinely mirthful. He placed one hand to his brow in a gesture of despair and muttered, "I do believe you are losing your mind, old boy." He dropped his hand, staring directly at his older sibling. "The actress. The Swan. That woman of low morals you have had the gall to place beneath Grandmother's very nose. While I admire your ever-increasing belief that you are supreme ruler of this particular corner of Britain, I cannot help but wonder at your sanity."

Tristan gave him an incredulous expression. "Are you suggesting that Lady Rachael is a woman of ill-repute? Where came you by this information?"

"What information?" He drew the words out as if the duke were incapable of understanding the king's English. "I know that woman, brother. Intimately, you might say. She is an actress or I'll eat my hat."

"I hope you enjoy that, Grey, because she is not an

actress." He saw the way Greyden pinched his thumb and middle finger of his right hand together and a smile crossed his face. "And you have never known her...intimately, Grey. Don't make a fool of yourself by inventing tales of your male prowess."

Greyden folded his arms over his chest and gave the duke a pitying look, shaking his head sadly. "If you believe her lies, you are a bigger fool than even I thought."

The duke returned his brother's look. "It is so sad to see a young man so twisted by his own greed and jealousy. You will, I hope, treat Lady Rachael with respect, Grey. If you do not, I will toss you out without a farthing and you can fend for yourself."

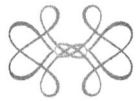

Everyone met in the drawing room for dinner that evening. Raven had stayed in her rooms for the rest of the day, pleading a sick headache and had been excused from the family's activities. She decided to meet them for dinner, however, as she couldn't very well hide in her rooms forever and had to face Lord Greyden at some point.

She left her rooms on the third floor with her head high. She was a lady, after all, or at least knew very well how to act the part. She felt the customary surge of excitement that occurred before a large role and smiled in anticipation. It was not often that she was able to use her skills directly on members of the upper class. She was looking forward to it immensely.

She had just reached the third floor landing and was gazing with a certain amount of wonder at a landscape scene that had caught her eye when Lord Windhaven stepped out of his rooms. Raven looked up and blushed at the look in his eyes. Her blush quickly turned to a smile of welcome. She had already forgiven him for his insulting offer earlier and now, as he was her only real ally in this farce, she was relieved to see him.

"My dear Lady Rachael," he murmured, clasping her hand and raising it to his lips. He pressed an intimate kiss into her palm, a tiny smile lighting his eyes as he gauged her reaction. "May I say how very enchanting you look this evening?"

"If I say no, sir, will you cease this flummery?" she asked facetiously, trying very hard to moderate her breathing.

"I will not," he declared, straightening and tucking her hand through his arm. "I am a duke, you know, and it was pointed out to me recently that I am lord of the manor and all that and I am supreme ruler of this tiny corner of Britain. I think that gives me the right to speak my mind, don't you agree?"

"I will not agree to that, my lord duke," she responded tartly. "You have much too high an opinion of yourself as it is. I will not add to it."

"Very well," he sighed. "I will just have to continue to

puff myself up. It will be difficult, but…"

"I'm sure you will manage, your grace," she finished for him.

Tristan looked down at her and smiled warmly. "I will manage, Rae, but I will manage much better with you by my side."

Raven's heart nearly stopped beating at the look in his eyes. He seemed so sincere, so true, that she had to remind herself that this was an act for them both and that were he not a duke, he would be the next Edmund Kean.

"If you are quite through," demanded the haughty voice of Lady Freya Cramshaw, "perhaps we can actually get somewhere."

"Freya," said the duke with a long-suffering sigh, his eyes directed heavenward as if begging some unseen entity to give him strength, "you would try the patience of a saint."

"Thank you, Tris, for that unwanted opinion," she snapped back. She stood there as if unsure of what to do or say next. Raven and Tristan just watched her, both equally curious to see what her decision would be.

"What are you gawking at?" she asked Raven insolently, her beautiful blue eyes filling with contempt.

"Freya," warned the duke.

"It's all right, Tristan, really," reassured the actress with an understanding smile. "I was just as precocious when I was twelve."

"I am not twelve!"

Raven affected surprise mixed with chagrin at her error. "I am so sorry, Lady Freya. How old are you? Thirteen?"

Tristan bit back a laugh at the outrage that settled on his sister's features. He kept silent, vastly diverted and wondering where this potentially explosive situation was going.

"I am sixteen, for your information," Freya informed her haughtily, her manner and expression reminiscent of their grandmother at her loftiest.

"You are?" Raven looked up at Tristan, seeking confirmation of this startling claim. Her look of amazement was superb. She gave Freya a pitying, consoling look and asked, "Are you sure? I have met many young ladies of that age, my dear, and none were quite so...young as you appear to be. Perhaps you are mistaken in your assumption."

Freya stared at Raven in speechless fury for a full five seconds before spinning on her heel and flouncing from their presence. The skirts of her yellow muslin gown swung angrily around her ankles, seeming to radiate their owner's fury.

"I apologize, my lord," Raven said softly, her throaty voice causing odd tremors in his middle. "I should not have baited her so. It was very ill-done of me."

"Nonsense," he responded briskly, wondering why he was being effected by her voice now. "That young lady was badly in need of a proper setdown and I think you did splendidly. Congratulate yourself on a stellar performance."

"I agree," Lord Greyden remarked snidely from behind them. "It was, indeed, a splendid display of superior thespian skill."

"Thank you," replied Raven evenly. "It is always nice to have one's accomplishments praised." She moved away from Tristan with a smile of welcome on her face that Tristan didn't like one bit.

She offered her hand and continued, "You must be Lord Greyden. I have heard much about you, sir."

"Nothing good, I'm sure," he said, his face reflecting his disbelief and contempt.

"On the contrary," she said, all pretty surprise. "Tristan has been praising you superior palate for wines. It is a subject in which I am vastly interested. My father owns a vineyard in France, you know, and I am eager to learn all about it."

Greyden's supercilious expression wavered a bit. Tristan saw nearly all his brother's doubts flee at this odd bit of insight. He wondered where Raven had learned about Greyden's almost obsession with wines. Tristan had not told her.

"I would be delighted to tell you all I can, Lady Rachael," Greyden finally said, clearly torn by what he knew to be the truth and what was presented as truth. "Unfortunately, my knowledge of the beginning processes is not what I would wish. I am just starting my own education in the hope of one day owning my own vineyard."

Tristan stared at his brother. "Why have you never told me, Grey? I would have put up whatever funds you needed to get started."

The younger man shrugged, completely off-kilter by all that had passed in the last few moments. He gave them both a rather odd look and suddenly walked off, his normally confident stride somewhat lagging.

Chapter Five

Raven's heart stopped beating. "Excuse me?" she asked, trying desperately to mask her sudden panic.

"Your father, dear. I expect he will arrive shortly," the dowager repeated patiently. "I cannot imagine him allowing you out of his sight for long. It has, after all, been over twenty years since you disappeared."

Raven smiled slightly. "Indeed, your grace. How true," she murmured. She shot Tristan the merest glance before adding, "He does not, however, wish to impose upon your hospitality, your grace, by inviting himself to stay."

She knew she'd made a mistake when she saw the look on the duke's face. He smiled disarmingly at his grandmother, saying, "Of course, he wouldn't dream of intruding when Rachael and I are only just getting to really know each other." He ignored the snort that came from his brother's direction and continued. "Perhaps in a few weeks he will join us. I did issue an invitation that he was quick to decline."

He marveled at how easily the lie rolled off his tongue. And, judging by the astonished look in his "betrothed's" eyes, she was just as amazed. He shrugged and turned to her. "Did he not, my love?"

Raven smiled. "Of course, my love." The emphasis on the endearment told him how she felt far more accurately than the sugary sweetness of her expression. She turned her attention back to her plate as the smile disappeared.

Tristan looked around the table, noticing that everyone's attention had focused on one another. His gaze halted on his brother who was staring at Raven as though she were a particularly succulent sweetmeat. He stifled the insane urge to pummel Grey to death and turned back to his now silent dinner partner.

"Rae, you have nothing to worry about," he assured her softly.

Her head snapped up, dark eyes suddenly blazing. "It was too close, your grace," she hissed just below a whisper, smiling falsely to appear as if all was well. "Have you considered what will happen to me when, and I place emphasis on when because it is inevitable, I am found out?"

Tristan blinked in the face of such intense anger. "I hardly think that is going to happen, my dear," he replied.

Raven's smile vanished and she turned fully to face him. Her black brows rose in an expression of surprise. "Oh, do you think so? How can you be so damn sure?"

The room's sudden silence alerted her to the fact that her voice had risen considerably on the last word. Her face flamed in embarrassment. For a moment, she had lost her temper, forgotten her surroundings, and let her fear come to the surface.

Too horrified to even meet the eyes of her host, she mumbled an excuse and fled the room.

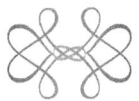

Tristan's thoughts were preoccupied the next few days. He puzzled over the situation he'd created, pondered all the possible ramifications of his actions, and realized that Raven was right. Of course they'd be found out. Of course it would come to light that he'd lied to his family and worse, hired an actress to impersonate a peeress.

What this would mean to him was moot. He could handle the stigma of eccentricity that would result. What was unacceptable was Raven's potential fate. He knew it would cause an uproar, particularly if Dunston discovered what they'd done.

It would be so bad, in fact, that he would be unable to help her in spite of his title. The duke slammed his head down on his desktop in a singularly un-dukely gesture of anguish.

Dear God, what had he been thinking?

While Tristan hid out in his study claiming an overwhelming amount of estate business, Raven avoided all potential confrontations by claiming a sick headache. She stayed in her room, allowing no one but Meg access. Not that anyone else actually tried to see her. But if they had, she would not have hesitated to turn them away.

Finally, three days after her loss of temper, Raven was sitting in the window seat staring out at the frozen lake down below. She had the sudden urge to go outside and let the brisk January air clear the cobwebs from her head. Without bothering to ring for Meg, she donned her warmest gown, grabbed up her heaviest cloak, and headed out the door. She somehow managed to make it outside without encountering anyone.

"Thank God," she muttered under her breath.

With long, graceful strides, Raven made her way to the lake, determined to explore at least that far. She had to do something or she'd lose her mind. She was still amazed that she'd let her fear show in a fit of temper. It was unlike her to lose her composure to such an extent. She hadn't even known she was afraid until the words had left her mouth. Why had she agreed to such an insane undertaking in the first place?

The answer to that was simple. Tristan Cramshaw, Duke of Windhaven.

From the moment she had seen him, she was far more than simply intrigued by his request. She found herself entertaining thoughts that she'd managed to keep firmly at bay for nearly two years. After accepting the protection of two different men, having her heart broken by the second and nearly losing her mind because of it, she'd promised herself that she would not weaken again. Yet, one look at the Duke of Windhaven had her wondering what kind of lover he was. Would he be tender and sweet or a little rough and wild? The desire to find out was great within her and she wondered how long it would be before she simply lost control and asked him to show her.

Damn. Would she never learn?

And to make matters worse, the duke's brother, Lord Greyden, was there to make life difficult for her.

As if conjured, Lord Greyden appeared from the back of the manor and approached. Raven groaned inwardly and pasted a welcoming smile on her face.

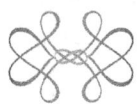

He wasn't sure what made him look out the window, but he did. And he stopped breathing. His blood ran cold through his veins. His hands trembled and he had to swallow around a large lump in his throat. The feeling of helpless panic didn't ease until he saw his brother walking out to meet Raven by the lake.

Tristan drew in a shaky breath and slowly let it out. He forced his mind away from the panic, away from the fear. With a shake of his head, he managed to firmly place the haunting images in the back of his mind. He fisted his hands tightly and slowly released his grip, relaxing them as much as possible.

Then he looked away. Perhaps he would have been better able to fight the panic had he simply looked away in the first place. It had been nearly impossible, however, to tear his eyes away from the beautiful woman standing on the edge of the frozen water. The thought of her stepping out on the ice was enough to make him scream. The possibility of her falling through the ice was uppermost in his thoughts.

He dared to look again and was relieved to see Grey leading her firmly away from the water's edge. His relief turned swiftly to annoyance then anger as he saw Grey take Raven's arm in a steely grip. She visibly pulled away only to stop when he bent closer and whispered in her ear. If the sudden pallor of her skin was anything to go by, Tristan would say she'd just been threatened. And by a member of his own household!

Slamming a fist onto the desk, Tristan strode from the room.

"What you ask simply isn't possible," Raven insisted, pulling again at Lord Greyden's solid grip. "Let go."

Grey gave her a little shake. "All I want is a little of what my brother's getting, my dear. What is so difficult about that?" he purred.

Raven forced her body to relax, smiling sweetly. "Oh, is that all? Why didn't you say so in the first place?"

Grey eyed her suspiciously. "So you will come to my room tonight?"

"Whyever would I do that?" Raven asked, feigning incomprehension.

Grey's confusion was apparent in the way he blinked twice at her before forming a careful reply. He opened his mouth to speak, then thought better of it and snapped his jaw shut. "Excuse me?" he finally ventured.

Raven nearly laughed. Instead, she pasted an innocent expression on her face and explained. "You said you expected to receive the same thing from me as your brother. I agreed. After all," she shrugged, "it really is not all that difficult to speak with a gentlemen."

"You cannot be serious," sputtered Grey after a moment of stunned silence. "You don't really expect me to believe you haven't been warming my brother's bed? That he keeps his mistress under grandmama's nose merely for her conversational abilities?"

"She is not my mistress, Grey."

Both turned in surprise at the softly uttered words. Raven smiled politely, masking her unease. Grey glanced from one to the other in patent disbelief.

"You bring an actress here and expect me to believe she's just a friend?" he sneered.

Tristan turned pale green eyes on his younger sibling. "I really don't care what you believe, Grey. Just remember who is duke and who is not. I will do what I damn well please in my own home. And whether or not my guest is indeed an actress need not concern you."

Greyden just stared at them for long tense moment before finally turning on his heel and moving furiously back to the house.

Raven turned to her "fiancé." "That was unnecessary, Tristan. I had the situation under control."

His look was disbelieving. "Did you? It appeared to me that my brother was about to threaten your virtue."

Raven pretended not to hear the slight emphasis placed on his final word. She gazed at him steadily, almost daring him to say more.

She involuntarily shivered. Tristan's entire manner changed. "Good God, woman! Why didn't you say you were near frozen? Come back into the house."

Raven allowed herself to be led back indoors. She was divested of her outer clothing and herded into a saloon with a brightly burning fire.

Tristan pushed her towards a chair and rang the bell for tea. When it arrived, he laced hers liberally with brandy and forced her to down every drop.

"Now, tell me what the blazes you were doing out there, anyway?"

Raven stared at him, almost bewildered at the past half-hour of flurried events. She shook her head, set aside her teacup and struggled for a measure of her habitual calm.

"I was merely enjoying the mild weather when your bother happened upon me. I did not purposely meet him if that is what you were implying."

It actually wasn't. The thought had never even entered his mind. He was still shook up from seeing her so close to the water's edge.

"I was implying nothing of the kind. You have an overactive imagination, madam."

She smiled. "I admit I do. It is an asset at times."

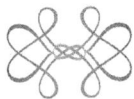

Chapter Six

There was an added guest besides Lord Greyden for dinner that evening. Reverend Mooney had been invited just that afternoon to join them. He was always a popular guest. He was witty, pleasant, and not too fawning. Tristan found himself at ease when in the other man's presence.

The duchess, however, was looking mightily pleased with herself. Tristan was convinced something was up and he was equally sure he wasn't going to like it. How long would he have to wait before his grandmother decided to share her plans with them all?

It was just after the last course was cleared away and the port was brought out that the duchess decided to make her announcement. Everyone watched, startled, as the old woman ordered all the servants to leave.

"I have invited the good reverend here for a specific purpose, my dears."

Tristan felt every muscle in his body stiffen. He glanced at Raven and noticed her own expression was far from easy.

"He has agreed to perform a wedding, at short notice, between my grandson, Windhaven and Lady Rachael."

"Absolutely not!" roared the duke before he could think better of it. The haughty look of disapproval he received from the duchess went ignored. "I will not be forced into marriage."

A look of confusion crossed the features of the other dinner guests. Why would the duke consider himself forced when he was to wed the girl anyway?

That exact thought entered Tristan's mind a second too late. He realized then how very insulting his words had truly been to his "fiancée." He turned to see her reaction to all this and was astonished at her look of utter composure. How could she remain so calm under these circumstances? Was she human?

"Perhaps Lord Windhaven and I should speak privately, your grace," Raven said then into the stunned silence.

In moments, Tristan found himself whisked from his grandmother's presence and into a small antechamber. Raven only released him after pushing him down into a chair. He stared at her while she poured him a glass of brandy and pressed it into his hand.

"Why are you so calm?" he finally demanded after downing the fiery liquid in one gulp.

"Her announcement was not wholly unexpected, Tristan. It came earlier than anticipated, to be sure, but it was still something she was expected to do. Why do you lie to yourself?"

Her question nearly made him choke on his third glass of brandy. "What the devil do you mean by that? I haven't been lying to myself."

"But you have," she pointed out reasonably. "You have convinced yourself that you can get out of this fictional engagement with no interference from your grandmother. You believe she would never dare to dictate your life when every action on her part has done just that. Why do you refuse to acknowledge this?"

The Duke of Windhaven dropped his eyes to his glass suddenly. He was afraid he might cry at this very real assessment of his life. What kind of man was he to allow an old woman to arrange every nuance of his existence? Was he a man at all?

Tristan slumped back down into his chair, dropping his head into his hands. How was he to avoid this newest direction his grandmother had taken with his life?

"It's no use, you know," murmured his companion kindly. Even in this moment of turmoil, her throaty voice could still affect him in a purely physical way.

"What is no use?" he forced himself to respond, lifting his face to gaze at her.

She gave a Gallic shrug. "This charade. We may as well confess and have the whole thing over with. I will return to London, hopefully of my own volition and not in chains, and we will forget we ever met."

The duke was surprised at the painful feeling her words gave him. Forget they had ever met? Not bloody likely!

His face brightened considerably as a new thought suddenly occurred to him. They could simply go through with the ceremony. She would sign her name to the marriage license and so would he. It would not be valid, however. The license would say Lady Rachael Eliot…

Decisively, he stood. "Come, we must inform the family of our decision."

Raven, a little taken aback at his sudden control, merely nodded and placed her hand on his arm. She knew her features showed complacency but inside, she was quaking with fear. These people had the power to have her taken up on charges. She didn't for a second believe some of them wouldn't jump at the chance to do so.

They re-entered the dining room to find everyone had remained exactly where they had left them. The duke signaled for everyone's attention and Raven braced herself for the expected ridicule and remonstrations.

"Grandmother, family. Rachael and I have discussed it and agree to marry on the morrow."

At his words, Raven did the unthinkable. She fainted.

"Something tells me your intended bride was of a different mind altogether."

Tristan glared at his brother. "She was simply overcome by the heat, you nodcock."

Greyden snorted derisively at that. "In the middle of January, brother? At least do me the courtesy of inventing something more plausible than the heat. I assure you, grandmother will not believe such a sorry excuse for a second. She may even determine the real reason behind your little bird's distress."

"And what is that?"

Tristan wasn't surprised when his brother suddenly remembered something of import requiring his attention elsewhere. Tristan was tempted to do the same but he knew the futility of running. The duchess would simply follow him and wait until he was done.

He turned to face the dame. "Madam?" he inquired politely.

"Do you think to ignore my question, Windhaven?"

He sensed amusement in her question but was at a loss to determine the source of her hilarity.

"Of course not, grandmother. I merely wonder at your asking it."

She chuckled. "I was eavesdropping, my boy. Greyden

mentioned my finding out the truth. I was simply wondering if you might be willing to tell me and thus save me distressing amounts of work and worry."

The duke smiled slightly. "I will refrain, madam, since I know how you like a good mystery."

The old woman grinned at that. "I do indeed, my boy. I do indeed."

Tristan cocked his head at her, eyes narrowing suspiciously. "How did you manage a Special License, madam?"

"I sent to London for that when you announced your engagement." At the duke's look of shock, she chuckled. "Do you take me for a fool, boy? I know my grandchildren and you will never marry if I don't put my foot down. We can't have that brother of yours inheriting the Duchy of Windhaven. He'd drag the whole of it through the mud before you were cold in the ground. Your tenants deserve better."

A low groan from the bed alerted the room's occupants to the possibility of yet another eavesdropper. Tristan hurried over, sitting gently on the edge of the bed.

"Ra-Rachael." He prayed his grandmother didn't notice the way he stumbled over the name. "How do you feel?"

She groaned again. "Like I've been run over by a carriage. And you?"

He laughed lightly, favoring her with a smile. "I've been better," he admitted. "Grandmother has come to see how you go on."

It was then, he realized, that she remembered exactly where she was and what had happened.

"Oh, dear God," she whispered. "What have you done?"

"Are you asking me or God?" he asked facetiously.

She pinched his arm. "Do you realize what you've done?"

"I will go. Apparently, you still have some things to discuss," the duchess told them, her haughtiness back in place. She swept from the room, closing the door firmly behind her.

Raven sat up and opened her mouth to speak but was firmly shushed by her soon-to-be husband. "She's listening," he mouthed silently. He leaned closer, putting his lips against her ear. "She hopes to discover something," he whispered. "Don't say anything that might lead her to suspect the truth."

At that moment, Raven couldn't have said anything if her life depended on it. The sensation of his lips and breath moving against her ear was sending pleasurable little swirls of longing deep into her very being. It was all she could do to refrain from turning her head slightly and meeting those firm lips with her own.

The duke pulled away slightly and gave her an odd look. She could only assume he had asked her a question and, ninnyhammer that she was, she had no idea what. What did this man have that made her forget her practiced ease and composure?

"I am sorry. What did you say?"

"I asked if you would be averse to telling the duchess that you are expecting as an excuse for your faint."

Raven wondered how many more shocks she would undergo before this nightmare was over. She hated to admit it, but Adam was right. Coming here had been insane.

"Of course I am," she told him hotly. He clapped a hand over her mouth before she could go on to tell him what she really thought of his ridiculous excuse.

"Gently," he admonished. He continued to hold her silent as he repeated his earlier words. "If we tell her we anticipated our vows and you are now *enceinte*, she will stop worrying about your odd fainting spell. We can marry and when it comes out that you are not, we can merely shrug it off as a mistake."

He finally released her and she sputtered, "The whole idea is preposterous. One day, my identity will be revealed and it will come out that we are not truly married. Then what will you do, Lord Windhaven? Will you be the first in line to say you were duped right along with your family and offer me up for the hangman's noose? Please tell me now so I know the proper action to take to save my own miserable neck."

Tristan was truly astonished at her vehemence. He felt his own temper rise at her words. He stood up, staring down at her. "Do you think that little of me, of my honor?

Do you honestly believe I would let anything bad happen to you? What have I done to make you think such a thing of me?"

"You have lied to your family, your grace. You have brought me here under false pretenses for the selfish reason of avoiding parson's mousetrap. You have ignored honor more than once during this fruitless endeavor. How can I think you wouldn't prove as selfish at the end of all this and offer me up as the sacrificial lamb to your precious honor?"

She was right. Good God, how had he gotten so mixed up? He was thirty-four years old. He knew better.

But how could they turn back now? And the bottom line was, he wanted this woman more than he had ever wanted anything in his life. Ever since the first time he'd seen her, he had dreamed of having her. He couldn't let her go now, no matter how selfish his motives seemed.

"What would you have me do, Rae? Should I march up to my grandmother right now and confess? What do you think she will do? Do you honestly think she would let you go peacefully? No, she won't. And I don't know that I could save you from her wrath." He crouched down beside her, pleading with her to heed him. "Give me this and I will come up with a way to release you, I promise. Just let me tell her now what I think is best and I will make everything right in the end. Please."

It was just plain stupid of her and she knew it. But she found it impossible to resist the entreaty in his beautiful green eyes. With a heartfelt sigh of resignation, she lay back down on the bed. "Very well, my lord duke. Do as you see fit. I place my life in your oh so capable hands from this day forward."

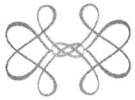

Chapter Seven

The wedding the next day was over before Raven had a chance to realize it. Had she really been complaining to Bri a mere two weeks ago that she was bored? She could use some boredom now. Things had gotten completely out of control and if there was anything she hated, it was not being in control.

And now, far from being in control, she had the urge to scream out her frustration until everyone sat up and took notice. Instead, she pressed her long fingernails into the arm of her "husband," taking great pleasure in the tensing of his muscles when she pressed particularly hard.

Apparently having had enough, Tristan grabbed her hand with his free one and squeezed hard enough to release her grip on his arm. The smile never left his face as he nodded to impromptu guests and whisked her out of the room.

Pulling her a short ways down the hall, Tristan shoved open a door, closing it firmly behind them. Then he paced away from her, clenching and unclenching his fists.

Raven was surprised at how perturbed he appeared. She watched him in total fascination while he got his emotions under control.

That was when she noticed his waistcoat.

"Is that blood?"

He looked at her. "What?"

"Your waistcoat has golden hearts—actual gold thread, I've little doubt—pierced with black arrows, the points of which are dripping blood. I was inquiring as to the authenticity of the blood."

He ignored her query and returned to the discussion at hand.

"I realize you are entitled to a lot due to what I am putting you through," he finally told her sternly, "but would it be too much to ask that you wait until our guests leave before inflicting physical injury on my person?"

Raven almost smiled. Almost. He was far angrier than her meager actions warranted. What on earth had him in such a pother?

In the space of two seconds, Raven decided to play with the man. In less time than that, she became someone else entirely.

With a sultry laugh, the actress turned peeress glided over to her partner in crime and smiled seductively up at him. Placing one hand on his broad chest, she had to take a deep breath to restore her equilibrium. Goodness, the man was solid!

"Tristan, darling, what has you in such a mood? Are you regretting your married state already?" Her voice was something she could manipulate to a nicety. She knew exactly what the deeper timbre of her voice could do to a man.

Tristan, however, refused to be manipulated. He wrenched her hand away from his person, growling an oath she had only heard used at the theater once when a stagehand dropped a heavy piece of the set on his foot. With a practiced twist, the duke brought both her hands together behind her back, yanking her close enough to feel his heartbeat against her chest.

"Do not poke fun at the devil, Raven. You know not what you incite with your actions."

Unafraid and actually surprised at the idea, Raven chuckled low in her throat. "I know exactly what I am doing, my lord duke. Or have you forgotten what I am?"

"I have forgotten nothing," he groaned and crushed her lips beneath his.

With little more than a token protest, Raven gave herself up to the feelings invoked by her "husband's" kiss. It was only when she felt cool air and a warm hand brush her bared breasts that she came back to the present and realized exactly what she'd allowed…no, caused, to happen.

"No."

It came out as little more than a squeak. With a forceful shove, she managed to make it come out a bit louder, loud enough to penetrate the sensual fog permeating the duke's brain. He backed away, breathing heavily, cursing under his breath. Then he stomped over to the window and threw it wide.

"I warned you, woman," he managed to mutter after several moments spent pacing before the open window. "I told you not to poke at the devil and what do you do? You mask yourself in your best harlot routine and proceed to do just that. Do you realize how tempting it was to ignore your request to stop and simply take you right here on the floor? Damn you, woman!"

Although hurt by his less than subtle way of telling her he found her conduct wanting, she felt the urge to laugh. If she didn't know better, she'd think his problem all along had been simple sexual frustration.

The thought occurred to her that she could rid him of that very easily…and enjoy doing it. But her days of loose living were over and while no one would think anything of them indulging—the world did think they were married, after all—she knew the truth and it would haunt her for the rest of her life.

Much in the way Levi haunted her. Only this time, she knew instinctively, would be much worse.

"And that doesn't help, you know."

Raven came to with a start…then flushed crimson when she realized she had neglected to right her appearance. With a strangled oath of her own, she turned her back on Tristan and struggled to pull her bodice back into place.

Freya walked into the room, gave them a disgusted look as if she knew what had just happened, and snapped, "Grandmother sent me to tell you to return to the party. She doesn't seem to want the guests thinking you are off somewhere f—"

Her words were suddenly cut short as her oldest brother tackled her and roughly shoved her back through the open door. He shoved her down the corridor and turned back to his bride. "Return when you can comport yourself with at least a semblance of dignity, Raven."

Raven was tempted to throw something at him but the door closed too quickly to give in to her desire.

As she moved toward the door, she realized he'd called her Raven. And she had little doubt his young sister had heard every word he'd said to her.

She was not looking forward to the results of his *faux pas*.

Taking a stroll in the early morning air had become a

favorite pastime of Raven's. She found it successfully
cleared the cobwebs from her brain after a night spent
wishing for things she could never have. And by making
the lake her destination each day, she could avoid her
"husband."

Her time was usually spent in determinedly ignoring the
urgings of her heart and body, while contemplating where
she should go from there.

Her meditations were interrupted by a commotion in the
front drive. Catching up her skirts, she hurried to see.

Shock and disbelief held her immobile when she
reached the front step. Tristan was standing there, watching
the proceedings with some interest. It was apparent he
didn't know who the arrivals were.

But Raven did. She barely had time to even
acknowledge the thought before Lady Brianna Prestwich,
Countess of Rothsmere, swept her into a hug. Oh, why
were they here?

Adam was a little more circumspect in his greetings,
satisfying himself with a mere kiss on the hand and an
inquiry as to her health. But Raven, knowing the dark-
haired man as well as she did, knew he was furious.

Tristan seemed most amused by it all. Raven wondered
how he'd feel when he learned just who his guests were.

Bowing to the inevitable, Raven made the introductions.
"My lord duke, may I make known Sir Adam Prestwich
and his wife, the Countess of Rothsmere? Adam, Bri, the

Duke of Windhaven…my husband," she added reluctantly.

Throughout, Raven watched Tristan's face and saw the exact moment he realized he was speaking to one of her former protectors. His green eyes turned suddenly chill and she knew he was about to disgrace them all by ordering the footmen to pack the carriage again, sending their guests on their way. Raven forestalled that by taking his arm and gaily inviting the couple inside.

"This is no time for petty jealousies, my lord," she murmured through her smiles as they led the way inside.

"Petty jealousies?" he gritted out. "Petty? Your audacity in inviting him here, madam, is what has me seething and nothing more. Why should I be jealous of him?"

Raven might have laughed at the very obvious jealousy her "husband" was displaying at that very moment if she didn't agree so wholeheartedly with his assessment. He possessed at least two inches and several pounds more muscle over Adam and was handsome enough to make any girl swoon. Adam had the kind of looks that appealed to the more daring girls, but Tristan was a god among men, a Greek Adonis. Raven shivered at the thought of actually possessing such a man.

"For your information, dear husband, I did not invite him. And even if I had, you needn't worry over our conduct."

Tristan snorted derisively. "You would endeavor to be circumspect, you mean? How very considerate of you, my dear."

The heavy sarcasm in his voice was not lost on Raven. She did ignore it, however, along with the sudden urge she had to do him a physical injury. "You have no reason to believe otherwise, my lord. You know what I am better than anyone." With that said, she turned and joined their guests in the drawing room.

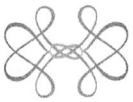

It was several hours later that Adam finally managed to get Raven alone. He was ready to tear somebody apart and he determined it would be best if it was the person whose actions had put him in such a foul humor in the first place.

He finally found her in the last place he thought to look —hiding in her bedchamber.

He entered without knocking, disturbing her at her bath. He did not let that stop him. She didn't possess anything he hadn't already seen, anyway.

"Just what the devil are you doing?" he snapped from less than two feet away.

Raven jumped but had to admit she wasn't really surprised. Adam could be the most tenacious person she knew when he had a bee in his bonnet about something. And her "marriage" to a duke was definitely a bee.

"Please sit, Adam," she offered dryly, waving carelessly towards the bed. "As you can plainly see, I'm bathing. Had you knocked first, as a gentleman ought, I could have informed you."

He waved that away and took up her invitation of a seat. "You're avoiding the blistering setdown I mean to give you. Which you rightly deserve, you foolish wench. What were you thinking to actually marry him?"

She sighed heavily. "I didn't, Adam. Not really."

He looked startled. "What do you mean, you didn't?"

"Just that. I signed the license as Lady Rachael. I didn't actually marry him."

He sat for two solid minutes, completely dumbfounded. "How could you do something so utterly stupid?" he finally uttered. He seemed almost defeated, something which Raven noted with some misgivings.

"It's not so stupid. I can walk away whenever I want, Adam."

He shook his head. "No, you can't, Raven. Windhaven owns you now just as surely had you actually married him. In fact, he has more control over your life than he ever did before."

Suppressing the shiver his words caused, she scoffed, "Nonsense! He assured me I can walk away when this is all over."

Adam continued to stare at her incredulously. "And just when is this all over, Raven? When he says so? The fellow's barmy and that's a fact. To have even proposed this escapade was insane and now he's proven he's not right in the upper works. And for you to have entered into it all so fully proves you are attics to let, too." He stood to leave. "I wish I could help you, Raven, and I promise I will do what I can when the time comes, but I have no good feeling about this."

Raven watched him leave, chilled by his words. He sounded as though she were facing her execution. But that was ridiculous. Windhaven would never let her die.

Would he?

At that moment, her door crashed open and Adam came hurtling back in. The duke stood in the open door, looking ready to burst.

Chapter Eight

Windhaven left his room just as Adam entered Raven's. He felt the now familiar surge of jealousy at the mere sight of his wife's former lover and turned resolutely in the opposite direction.

Then he stopped. And turned. And stared. What was Prestwich doing in Raven's room?

Determined to get to the bottom of this newest mystery, the duke stood outside Raven's door, listening unabashedly to the hushed conversation taking place within. He couldn't hear much, damn the thick oak doors. At one point he heard splashing, so he assumed Raven was bathing. Had Prestwich joined her? The mere thought nearly sent him crashing through the door. To think he had to pander to a guest who used to share his wife's bed when her own husband had yet to see her naked made Windhaven see red.

It was at this unfortunate point that Adam left the room. He managed to close the door before Tristan grabbed him by the lapels of his jacket and threw him against the opposite wall.

"Why were you in my wife's chamber?"

When he left Raven's room, Adam had been saddened by her new and very serious predicament, more so because of her apparent ignorance of her own problem. Now he was incensed.

He laughed in the duke's face as he angrily brushed away the larger man's hold. "None of your business, you miserable whoreson."

Tristan was taken aback by Adam's apparent anger. What had he to be angry about? He had a beautiful wife and mistress and apparently everything he'd ever wanted. It was enough to make a man seriously consider murder.

"She's not yours anymore, Prestwich. She's mine. Consider carefully if you think she's worth dying for."

Adam laughed again. Tristan felt a chill in the somewhat maniacal edge he heard in the other man's laughter.

"You risk her life with your silly charade and dare to ask me if I would die for her? You're the damned bounder who's going to get her hanged. But at least your family will stop hounding you about marrying."

Adam crashed back through Raven's door before the

final word had even left his mouth. He lay sprawled on the floor for all of two seconds before launching himself back at the furious duke.

Neither noticed the astonished Raven. She watched them try to beat each other to a pulp and was amazed that it was apparently over her. It might have actually been diverting had they not appeared to be serious in their goal of murder.

Rising with the utmost grace, Raven swept up an extra bucket of water as she moved closer to the feuding pair. One second later, they broke apart, sputtering and shaking water from their faces.

Raven stood, dripping and naked, gazing at them both with a blank expression. "If you gentlemen are quite finished, I would appreciate it if you left me to bathe in peace." She tossed the emptied bucket at them. "And be kind enough to see this refilled, if you please." And so saying, she turned and slipped gracefully back into the tepid water, looking at neither gentleman as she did so.

As the door closed softly behind her, Raven released the sob she'd held in check. And once released, one sob became many.

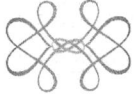

He heard her. They both did. Adam glared hard at the duke, drew back, and punched him square in the solar plexus. Windhaven bent over, gasping for breath.

"For making her cry."

The baronet walked away, anger emanating from every pore. Tristan slumped against the wall, sliding down until he sat on the floor. His anger had fizzled the second he had seen Raven standing there, magnificent in her nakedness, seething with anger but appearing as calm as if she were used to entertaining brawling gentlemen in her bedchamber.

He had been amazed at her composure. And now, he felt like the brute he undoubtedly was for making her cry.

And he'd been wrong. Oh, so wrong about her and Prestwich. He could tell from Adam's demeanor that Raven did not affect him in the least anymore. In fact, he seemed not to even see her as a woman, let alone one he'd made love to too many times to count.

Oh, to be the man to possess such beauty. She was more beautiful than he'd ever imagined. Her skin was flawless, perfect with a subtle Mediterranean olive cast. Her features were exotically cast with dark, slanted eyes and deep red lips. And her body...

Dear God, how Tristan wished he were actually able to call her his. The woman was a goddess. His desire to go back in there and make passionate love to her was so great he actually started to rise from his slumped position.

Then he heard a particularly bitter sob and thought his heart might break. What, exactly, had he done that so upset her?

Unfortunately, Greyden chose that moment to go to his own room to dress for dinner. He saw his brother and stopped abruptly. With one brow raised, he sauntered over.

"Evicted already, brother? Whatever have you done to offend the pretty actress?"

Tristan glared at his younger sibling. "I have told you she is not what you think, Grey. Why do you insist in believing otherwise?"

The younger man smirked. "I but suspected before, Tris. Now, I know."

The duke just stared at him, his face blank. His silence was question enough.

"You called her Raven. Freya overheard a certain conversation a few weeks ago and informed me, as she was worried something not quite right was in progress beneath our very noses."

Tristan grunted noncommittally. "And you believe the ramblings of a spoiled child bent on mischief?"

His reaction brought Greyden up short...momentarily. "Nonsense. I know what I know. And I just thought to let you know that your secret is safe with me. We are brothers, after all. And if one cannot trust one's own brother..."

He left it at that, and left Tristan in peace, for the moment. The duke knew his brother well enough to know he'd probably have demands later. He just wondered if he'd be able to meet them.

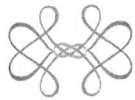

Two days later found Raven exploring the frozen lake. It

was so beautiful, pristine and sparkling. She was tempted to find a pair of skates and make use of her free time and the fine weather.

Adam and Bri were still visiting. There was a sort of tentative truce between Tristan and Adam but the tension was still palpable entity whenever they were in the same room. Raven almost wished the men would simply kill each other and leave the rest of them in peace.

Feeling the cold finally penetrate her wool cloak, Raven decided it was time to return to the manor. She entered a side door and made immediately for her room. She was in no mood to see any of the family. Greyden had been more offensive than usual and Freya was just as unpleasant as always. In the girl's manner, however, was an underlying note of contempt that Raven had trouble coping with. She avoided the girl as much as possible.

Her desire for solitude went unheeded. No sooner had she reached her chamber door than Lord Greyden accosted her. In no mood for his insinuations, she tried to get inside her room before he could actually stop her.

It was not to be. Her hand was on the door handle when he took her other arm in a firm grip. He brought her around to face him, a leering smile on his handsome face.

"Where have you been, little Swan?" he asked. "Meeting with your paramour? I admit I am surprised you have the audacity to take a lover beneath my brother's very nose."

Raven was startled to hear the way he addressed her. He seemed very sure of her identity. It would only a matter of time then before he started making demands.

Steeling herself against the desire to strike out at him verbally and physically, she replied steadily, "I don't know what you're talking about."

He laughed. Something in his laughter made her shiver despite herself.

"Do you not? I find that curious. You seem fairly intelligent after all and I was reasonably blunt, I'm sure. What part was beyond your comprehension?"

"The part where you insinuated Sir Adam is my lover. We are acquaintances, nothing more. His wife happens to be my dearest friend."

Thankfully, Bri chose that moment to enter the corridor. As if sensing something was amiss, she moved toward them with a smile pasted firmly on her beautiful face.

"Have you just come in, my dear?" she asked solicitously. "You must be nearly frozen. And here you stand in this drafty corridor. Come, let me help you." With a painfully sweet smile for the young lord, she steered Raven into the chamber, firmly closing the door behind her.

"And what, may I ask, was that young puppy up to?" she asked, helping Raven remove her heavy cloak.

"The usual. Threats, insinuations, impertinence. What else?" With somewhat jerky movements, a circumstance quite unlike her, Raven moved to the fire and stretched out her fingers to the pleasant warmth. She felt chilled to the bone and she knew it had nothing to do with staying out of doors too long.

"I'm not sure I can do this anymore," she murmured half to herself. "Everyday, Lord Greyden becomes more bold, Lady Freya becomes more insulting, and Tristan...dear God, how can any woman be around that man and not—" She broke off abruptly, staring morosely into the dancing flames.

"Kill him?" Bri offered helpfully.

Raven had to smile at that. Bri's near-hatred for men was legendary. There were few she actually called friends and even fewer she actually trusted. It was no surprise to Raven that Tristan fell into neither category.

"That wasn't exactly what I was going to say but I dare say it's close enough."

Bri moved forward and wrapped her arms around her friend. "I know what you meant, my dear. I'm sorry you have landed in this predicament. When did you realize you're in love with him?"

Raven's body jerked at the words. Bri sighed softly. "Oh, my poor dear friend. You didn't realize, did you? I'm so sorry." Her voice was gentle and soothing. Raven couldn't stop a tear from falling dejectedly. "But it's no use. He's a duke and you're..."

At that, Raven moved out of her friend's embrace. "I have dreams sometimes, you know," she said, almost conversationally, turning away from her friend. "Sometimes I dream that I really am this Lady Rachael and Tristan is madly in love with me and my future is bright. Then I wake to the reality of my situation. Far from being courted by a rich and handsome duke, I'm courting a hangman's noose."

Bri could say nothing. Indeed, what could one say to such a confession? She just stood there, available if her friend needed her.

The former actress laughed lowly. "It's amazing, is it not? I was once the greatest actress ever to tread the boards. And now...now I'm nothing but an upstart with pretensions above her station. I'm actually tempted to try to win a duke."

Turning back to face Bri, Raven gestured almost wildly, an action so unlike her that the other woman took a hasty step back.

"And do you know what? I won't survive this, Bri. I'll either be taken up or wither away and die from a broken heart."

"A little melodramatic, my dear, even for you."

The two women smiled at each other. Then Raven said, "I'm going to fight, Bri. I'm going to ask Adam for his help, if you don't mind."

All Bri could do was nod. She had a sick feeling in her stomach. Raven looked completely serene yet there was a crazed look in her eye that Bri couldn't like.

Raven was finally left alone. Turning back to the fire, she stared, unseeing, into the flames.

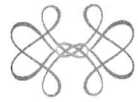

Chapter Nine

"You want me to what?"

Raven's expression revealed none of her annoyance. She merely gazed at her former protector, daring him to call her crazy.

"You heard me, Adam, and what's more, you fully understood. Will you do it?"

"You're asking me to investigate a duke and his family, looking for…dirt? What makes you think there is any to find?"

"A mere suspicion. I think Lord Greyden is the most likely one to have secrets. Start with him. I think he poses the greatest threat."

Adam's hands clenched at his sides and Raven suspected it had little to do with the cold.

They stood in the sunlight, close to the edge of the frozen lake. Raven knew it was a safe place to talk since Tristan held some sort of aversion for the place. The others had gone into the village on an outing and the duchess—the dowager duchess, Raven reminded herself—was off on her own doing God only knew what.

Showing not a sign of the chill that threatened to penetrate her very being, Raven waited for Adam's reply. He was good at ferreting out any kind of information one could ever want or need. She just hoped he'd be willing to help.

"Very well," he muttered darkly. "I'll do what I can since it may save your beautiful neck at the end of all this."

She smiled. "Thank you, Adam. I appreciate all you are willing to do for me."

He bowed a trifle mockingly. "My pleasure, dear lady. I will take my leave of you now and inform Windhaven"—the name was uttered with a shred of loathing—"that my family will be departing forthwith."

He turned to leave her but at the last second, he moved back and pulled her roughly into his arms, hugging her tightly. "Don't let anything happen to you while I'm gone, Raven."

She smiled into his shoulder, tears starting in her eyes. "I won't, Adam. I promise."

He released her, staring down at her with a great deal of affection. Touching her cheek lightly, he murmured, "After all, what kind of world would this be without the Ebony Swan?"

"I love you, Adam. Take care of the new baby. And tell Linnet I'll come for her soon."

She watched him go, sad at the imminent departure of her friends, but resigned.

Tristan had seen the whole disgustingly touching scene from his study window. He tortured himself with visions of the baronet and Raven together, wanting badly to beat Prestwich into a bloody pulp.

He nearly exploded at the sight of Adam hugging the actress. He could not go on like this. He would die of frustration or worse, hang for murder.

Resolved to have this over once and for all, the duke left his study. Upon entering the foyer, he realized Adam and his wife were directing servants to pack their things.

Forcing himself to remain calm, Windhaven approached the pair to find out what was going on.

Adam smirked at him. "Just the man I wanted to see. We are leaving. It is apparent we were never welcome in the first place. We shall trouble you no more."

Bri smiled at the duke with no less hostility than her husband did. "I would like to take Rae with us, but she insists on staying." Her expression turned a trifle melancholy. She stepped closer and whispered fiercely, "If you hurt her, duke or no, I will kill you."

Adam possessed himself of his wife's arm and pulled her away from the Duke of Windhaven. "Apologies, duke. My wife is very protective of her friends." His tone suggested the duke had best heed the warning of the pretty young woman.

Tristan just looked at them blandly. "I don't want to hurt her," he assured them quietly. He gave no indication that he paid any heed to Bri's warning or Adam's for that matter. He merely stated a fact and they could do what they wanted with that information.

He watched his guests leave an hour later. Relieved to finally be quit of them, he went looking for Raven, who had neglected to come in to see them off.

He found her on the lake. His heart tripped at the sight. He could barely bring himself within fifty feet of the frozen body of water. His horror at the sight of his "wife" out there, skating away as if nothing were wrong, was nearly enough to throw him into a panic of monumental proportions.

Unaware of what he was doing, he edged closer, screaming hoarsely, "Raven, no! Come back! Please!"

Startled to the point that she tripped, Raven looked around to see the urbane Duke of Windhaven on his knees, screaming at her with what appeared to be an unreasonable amount of alarm. He was a good twenty feet from the lake and reaching out towards her as if he could simply snatch her to him. He looked completely out of his mind.

Rising painfully to her feet, as she had managed to bruise her backside in her fall, Raven skated carefully to her "husband." Neglecting to first remove her skates, she nearly tripped again in her effort to reach the distraught man.

She fell to her knees before him, gathering him to her. He clung to her like a lifeline, crushing the breath from her, making her gasp.

"Tristan, my dear, what is it?" she pleaded. He merely squeezed her tighter. She groaned, wondering if this was how she was meant to die.

He reared back suddenly, his face a mask of angry worry. "Do not ever go on the lake!"

Startled beyond anything by his yelling in her face, she stumbled to her feet, completely forgetting about the skates still attached to her half-boots. She twisted her ankle painfully, falling against the duke as he rose with her. She cried out, trying to push away from him.

"Fool woman, stop! You'll only twist it more." His tone had gentled considerably and Raven's tension eased, but only a very little. This man was proving to be very unpredictable. And Raven hated unpredictability.

"Whatever is the matter with you?" she demanded. "Have you taken leave of your senses?"

Windhaven pushed her down into a sitting position, then dropped down before her. He ignored her question, removing her skates and tossing them carelessly aside for the servants to retrieve later. He probed at her ankle, his face screwed up in concern. "It doesn't appear too injured. We should get you back into the house."

Unable to do anything but allow him, Raven felt herself lifted in strong arms. The duke made short work of the return to the house, his long legs positively eating up the distance like nothing. He seemed unburdened by her not inconsiderable weight. He must have a magnificent physique.

The thought made her shiver unexpectedly. Her desire to become well known with that physique grew with each passing day in this man's company and she was unsure she'd be able to resist much longer.

He entered her room and set her gently on the bed. Meg came in from the dressing room, exclaiming over the sight of her injured mistress.

"Go get a cloth to wrap the ankle, Meg," the duke ordered. The maid swiftly complied, returning to hand her employer a sturdy bit of cloth she'd managed to procure from the housekeeper.

"Thank you, Meg. That will be all," Raven said firmly. The girl glanced at the duke, who nodded.

They were alone. Raven wanted to ask what had happened out there but something in the set of Tristan's shoulders warned her not to mention it.

Tristan quickly removed her boot and reached up beneath her skirt to remove her stocking. Her heart skipped a beat as he hesitated before finally sliding the thin garment down her smooth leg. Was it just her imagination or did his hand linger for a moment on her bare calf?

He cleared his throat as he tied off the bit of cloth. "That should hold your ankle fairly straight. Try to stay off it for a while. I will send for Doctor Murphy but he probably won't be here until tomorrow." He rose a trifle unsteadily to his feet. He moved to leave but Raven's voice stopped him in his tracks.

"Will you not tell me what is wrong?"

He wanted nothing more than to ignore her but something in her voice begged for understanding. He knew he couldn't possibly confess his abject fear of the lake. He could, however, appease at least part of her query with a little white lie.

"I had heard the lake was starting to thaw. I was worried."

Raven was an actress of phenomenal proportions. Hence, she could tell a lie when she heard one. And his actions by the lake had gone far beyond mere worry. He had been terrified and nearly hysterical.

But it was not time for confessions, she could see.

"Will you carry me down to dinner?" she asked instead.

The way his broad shoulders visibly relaxed, she knew

she had relieved his mind by avoiding what was obviously a painful subject.

It was yet another mystery Miss Raven Emerson was determined to solve.

On January 29, mad King George died. His son, the despised and adored Prince Regent, became King George IV.

The country was thrown into mourning and muted celebration. The new king immediately demanded a Bill of Divorce be granted him. And so began long tedious months of debate in the House of Lords, requiring the presence of virtually every titled man in Britain. Lord Windhaven managed a suitable excuse to beg off, citing family matters that could not be ignored. He was granted permission to stay home and tend to his family. It was probably helpful that Windhaven happened to be on rather friendly terms with the new king, as well.

The Duchess of Windhaven was particularly distraught over the whole matter. Her friendship with the queen was well known and, while she hadn't seen her friend in quite some time, she had kept up a faithful correspondence with the new king's mother.

She immediately departed for London escorted by her grandson, Lord Greyden.

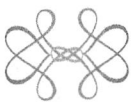

Chapter Ten

Adam was astonished and appalled and maybe even a little amused. What he'd discovered about Lord Greyden Cramshaw was not what he had expected. Far from it. He had expected to find the usual failings in a younger son, namely, dissipation, women, and gambling debts. What he'd found was much worse…or better, depending on one's point of view.

With a faint smile and a vague desire to see Raven's face when she discovered what he had, Adam began to pen a note…

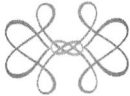

"Dear Rae, I have discovered something of no little

interest. I have it on the best authority—mine—that young Greyden has been keeping secrets. My dear, go to this address, and all will be revealed. A"

Raven made note of the address then set the vellum aside, wondering what on earth had Adam sounding almost giddy. It must be something particularly shocking but not necessarily vile. Adam would never send her somewhere dangerous so she had to assume this secret was scandalous rather than unnatural.

Wondering how she could go to the address indicated without drawing unwelcome attention or suspicion, Raven went for a walk. It occurred to her that she wasn't even sure where the place was located. Although the address was of a village she was sure was in the vicinity, she was unsure which direction or where to go once she reached it.

She started walking toward Lower Kempworth, just idling away her time, when she noticed the duke in his curricle. He pulled up beside her and doffed his hat.

"Care to go for a drive, wife?" he asked pleasantly.

The scene at the lake had not been mentioned between them again and they had gotten on in relative peace in the two weeks since. So, Raven smiled and accepted the hand he offered her.

Once settled, she pasted a benign look on her face and asked innocently. "Where is Speldhurst located? I heard one of the servants mention the place and I have to admit I've never heard of it."

He gave her a quizzical look. "It's just a little northwest of Tunbridge Wells. Did you want to go visit?"

Unsure whether he was speaking of Speldhurst or Tunbridge Wells, Raven declined. This was something she needed to do alone.

"Am I allowed to take Meg into Tunbridge Wells?" she asked, gazing over the white countryside.

Glancing a little uneasily at his companion, the duke nodded. "I don't see why not. It's a perfectly safe bit of road. When would you like to go?"

"Oh, I have no definite plans," she said, smiling. "I was just wondering what was acceptable to you and what wasn't."

They lapsed into preoccupied silence, the duke wondering why she wanted to go into Tunbridge Wells without him and Raven wondering how she was to manage to distract him long enough to get there without alerting him to that fact. She supposed she could actually take Meg as she'd implied. The girl would not give her away and she needn't know exactly what Raven discovered in Speldhurst.

Her opportunity came two days later. The day was pleasantly sunny. Raven decided she needed some things that weren't available in Lower Kempworth. Enlisting Meg's assistance, they were soon ensconced in the carriage with hot bricks at their feet and warm lap robes over their knees for there was still a slight chill in the air.

They arrived in Tunbridge Wells. Raven and Meg spent

an hour or so window shopping and making little purchases. The town was beautiful, a sort of spa frequented by the nobility. Raven was uncomfortable there, afraid someone might recognize her as the Ebony Swan.

As quickly as possible without alerting her companion to her unease, she returned to the carriage, ordering the driver to continue on to Speldhurst. Meg gave her an odd look but remained unusually silent.

The coach stopped outside a hostelry. The two women stepped down. Raven turned to the coachman and inquired about a certain street. He pointed west and Raven smiled, thanking him.

Raven then turned to her maid. "Please stay with the carriage, Meg. I will return presently." The maid complied with a worried little frown between her brows.

A few minutes later, Raven stood outside a pleasant little cottage, small by any person's standards, and wondered what she was about to discover. It was nerve-wracking, to say the least, not knowing what one was walking into.

She knocked. And waited.

Perhaps it was just her nervousness but it seemed to take forever before someone finally opened the door.

She nearly fainted at the sight of the child standing before her. He was angelic in appearance, with brown hair and gray eyes. In fact, he had the look of—

"Matt!"

Another small being ran towards them, falling down at

Raven's feet. She stooped to help the child up, beholding blond hair and dark blue eyes. The boy grinned, kissed her cheek and ran back the way he had come.

Raven rose, ready to ask the other boy if she could see his mother or father when yet another child came up. She was a pretty thing who appeared to be no more than thirteen or so with light brown hair and beautifully wide violet eyes.

"Can I help you?" this newest arrival asked politely.

Raven smiled in some relief. She was forming a few conclusions and wanted some answer. Perhaps this child could help her.

"I am..." she hesitated slightly. "Miss Eliot. Can I speak to your mother or guardian?"

The girl frowned. "You can talk to my sister. She's in here."

Raven followed into a pleasantly cramped little receiving room. Sitting in a chair with some mending in her lap was an ethereal creature with white blond hair and the palest gray eyes Raven had ever seen. Her smile was welcoming even while it was inquiring.

She rose to her feet, showing herself to be a few months gone in pregnancy. Raven smiled, offering her hand in greeting.

"I am Miss Eliot. How are you? Please sit back down," she implored, firmly stifling the pitiful jealousy she felt. She hadn't realized until that very moment that she wanted children of her own.

Sinking back to her previous position, the woman smiled in return, saying, "It is a pleasure to meet you, Miss Eliot. I am Mrs. Greyden Cramshaw."

Meg was getting worried. Her mistress had been gone for well over an hour. She wondered what kind of trouble she'd be in when his grace discovered where they had gone. She could lose her position.

A sigh of relief escaped her when she saw her grace returning to the inn. The smile on the beautiful duchess's face was bemused in Meg's humble opinion.

The lady disappeared from the maid's view for a moment as she entered the inn. In moments, she joined Meg in the private parlor the innkeeper had shown her into over an hour before.

Removing her bonnet and placing it on a chair near the crackling fire, Raven grinned in a totally unguarded way. "I have just met the most wonderful young woman, Meg. I wish I could have taken you with me. She was the loveliest creature I have ever seen. Almost unearthly."

Meg had a strong inclination to cross herself—and she wasn't even Catholic. "How so, your grace?" she asked politely.

"Silver hair and eyes, willowy figure. Everything I've always wished to be," the black-haired siren admitted ruefully. She sank down into a chair, an almost dreamy expression on her face. "And she has the sweetest disposition." Her face suddenly contorted into something closely resembling outrage. "It makes me want to spit when I think of how…oh, never mind."

Turning and finally really looking at Meg, Raven said, "I am sorry I kept away so long, my dear girl. It won't happen again, I promise."

Little reassured by this statement, which implied this trip would be made again, Meg merely nodded in acceptance. What else could she do, after all? She was just the maid.

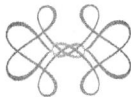

As soon as Raven was in the house, Tristan made for the stables. He found the coachman helping the stableboy unhitch the horses.

Feigning nonchalance, he approached the two men. "Hallo, Camp, William." They smiled at the greeting, having known the duke since he was a lad. "And where have you been this fine day." He made his way over to his own bay stallion, acting as though the horse was his sole reason for being in the stables.

The coachman nudged William. "We been into Speldhurst this day, yer grace."

Dropping the pose of indifference, Tristan approached his employees again. "Where in Speldhurst?"

Camp swallowed with difficulty at the intent look on his master's face. He informed the duke that he wasn't sure other than a street name. Then he offered up Meg as a sacrifice to the large man's curiosity.

Tracking Meg down was easier then he'd expected. She was just coming out of Raven's room on her way to get tea for her mistress.

"A moment, Meg."

The maid yelped, not having seen the duke. Turning to inquire after his pleasure, she sighed at the look on his face. Following in his wake, she entered a small room just off an empty bedchamber.

"Yes, your grace?" she asked politely.

"Where did you go this day, Meg?"

"With the mistress, your grace."

He smiled faintly. "And where did she go?"

"With me?"

"Meg. Your willingness to protect your mistress is commendable. But, please just answer the question."

The maid sighed. "She went to visit a lady on Grove Lane, your grace. And that's all I know. She didn't take me with her."

There was no help for it. He'd have to ask Raven. He dismissed Meg with a negligent wave of his hand. He followed her out the door shortly afterward.

Raven was reprieved of her husband's inquisition until after dinner. Some estate affairs had come up and kept him busy until that time.

With a polite excuse to the family, he escorted his bride to her room. She didn't try to prevent him from entering; in fact, she acted as though she expected him to enter.

A point she confirmed a moment later. "Before you start asking questions, Tristan, let me assure you there is little enough to tell and nothing for you to worry about."

"Whom were you meeting?" he asked bluntly.

She turned to face him. "What do you mean by that?"

He approached her, like a predator stalks its prey. "Who is he? Oh, I was informed you went to meet a lady but you and I both know that was just a cover for what you were really doing."

She felt like slapping him. "You are correct, your grace. How stupid of me to assume you would believe such a story. You are far more intelligent than that, are you not?" Her tone mocked him.

He felt like slapping her. "Who is he?" he asked again. He was close enough to smell her subtle fragrance, roses and woman. He grew incensed at the idea that she might be willingly giving to another man what he was entitled to as her husband. He deliberately ignored the voice that whispered she was no such thing.

"Get out," she said evenly.

She had donned her blandest expression, much like the

one he'd seen on her face when she'd calmly—and nakedly —broken up his fight with Prestwich.

That recollection succeeded in inflaming him more than he'd anticipated. Two parts anger and one part desire, Tristan lost control. He reached out to shake some sense into her but instead crushed her against his hard chest, smothering her protest in a heated kiss.

And Raven, angered beyond anything, met his passion and surpassed it. This was what she wanted. This man, this feeling, this heat. It was useless to protest; she'd never felt such a physical need for a man. It was all consuming, engulfing her in a tidal wave of desire for the fulfillment only he could give her.

And before she quite realized it, she was pressed into the bed, allowing Tristan full rein and even helping him. Within a matter of seconds, she was undressed, he was down to his breeches and she was ready to tear those off with her teeth.

Then he spoke. Pressing kisses along her neck and over her breasts, he murmured, "You are mine, Raven." Pausing briefly in his sensual onslaught, he stared down into her eyes, suddenly dead serious. "Don't you dare give yourself to another man ever again."

Desire fizzled and died a quick death, fury taking over like fire to a dry field. Raven released a shriek loud enough to wake the dead, bringing her elbow up in a wide arc. She caught the side of his face, knocking him momentarily senseless. He eased up a bit, much to her satisfaction and his painful mortification—she was able to bring her knee up into his groin with unerring accuracy.

Doubling up, the noble Duke of Windhaven tumbled from the bed, hitting the floor with a thump. He groaned, cupping himself protectively and seriously contemplating murder.

Raven was instantly repentant. She hadn't meant to maim the man, just gain her immediate release. She had that now and was unsure what to do for the man curled on her bedroom floor.

None of the men she'd ever treated in such a way had ever remained long enough for her to see what happened afterward. So now, sitting up on the bed with a sheet wrapped protectively around her nakedness, she instinctively knew that getting near him at the moment was likely to cause her own immediate demise.

She didn't realize how right she was. Tristan continued to hold himself, fighting a bout of unmanly tears and devising all sorts of foul tortures to visit upon the lovely body of the pseudo Duchess of Windhaven.

After five minutes of willing the pain away, Tristan was finally able to gasp out, "Unbelievable."

Raven, still seated on the bed watching him warily, replied, "What, my lord?"

"The fact," he retorted brokenly, "that you are still here. And not," he paused, "running for your life."

Surprising them both, Raven chuckled. "I have little to lose, my lord. And I have just been informed that you own me. I suppose my life is yours to do with as you will."

Struggling gingerly into a sitting position, the duke smiled, leaning his back against the bed. "I'm a jealous fool," he muttered. Turning his head slightly, he looked up at her. "A lady? Truly?"

Raven hesitated. "No. A married woman but technically not a lady."

Seemingly satisfied with this response, Tristan returned his gaze to the opposite wall. "I apologize, Rae. It was stupid of me to assume you were meeting a man in Speldhurst. Was it Grey's wife then?"

Raven stared in shock. "How did you know?"

He shrugged one well-muscled shoulder. "He thinks it's some great secret. I only wonder that he actually married the girl instead of following in our ancestors' footsteps. Trickery, you know." They shared a conspiratorial glance. "And how did you find the lovely wife? Is she well?"

"You have never met her?"

He shook his head. "No. I saw her once from a distance. A hauntingly lovely creature. Like an angel come to earth. I can understand Grey's desire to have her."

"Yes," murmured Raven with a little jealous pang of her own. "She is well. Increasing."

He looked up at that. "Again? This will make...what? Three?"

She nodded. It was apparent her "husband" had made his brother's family his business while not actually interfering.

"You've been providing for them when Grey conveniently forgets they exist, haven't you?"

He grunted at that. "I'm not as stiff-rumped as I appear. I have no problem with the girl's birth or breeding. I wish Grey would realize we would welcome her and act accordingly."

"She doesn't know who he is," she commented a little offhandedly. "She introduced herself as Mrs. Greyden Cramshaw."

A moment of silence ensued. Tristan frowned, then asked, "How did you find out about Lily?"

Raven hesitated. It would be wrong to implicate Adam in anything. The way the duke already felt about the other man was bad enough. To discover that that man had been spying on his family…

Looking down at her hands, she replied, "I just stumbled upon her, so to speak."

Tristan turned just enough to look clearly at her. "How does one just stumble upon something or someone who lives a good ten miles away?"

She shrugged, offering a radiant smile. "Servant's gossip?"

He snorted, letting it drop. He suspected he really didn't want to know anyway.

It struck neither Raven nor Tristan as odd that they were sitting, half-naked, discussing his family as if nothing of any moment had just occurred between them. If either one considered taking up where they had left off, they kept the thought to themselves.

Tristan doubted he could, anyway. He would probably be tender for days. The woman definitely knew how to protect herself.

At that he smiled. He needn't worry too much about her then, he thought as he carefully made his way across the corridor and into his own chamber. He hadn't bothered re-dressing himself and ignored the curious stare of his valet.

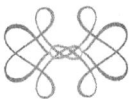

Chapter Eleven

Peace reined between the Duke and "Duchess" of Windhaven. Neither mentioned the night they'd lost control and both strove to maintain a rigid decorum both in and out of company.

This, of course, only aided in building the tension simmering just below the surface between them. Tristan took to more physical pursuits, hoping to exhaust himself by nightfall. Raven started unobtrusively avoiding him whenever possible.

It was into this odd arrangement that Lady Windhaven returned with her grandson firmly in tow. They were full of stories about an assassination plot uncovered by Lord Sidmouth.

Apparently, a certain group of men gathered, determined to murder the entire Cabinet and the new king, seize the Tower of London and the Bank of England, and set up a Provisional Government. One of their own people had been spying for Lord Sidmouth and reported the whole thing.

Greyden related with particular relish that five rebels were hanged and five more transported. Tristan shook his head in disgust. He honestly believed his brother was a little less than sane most of the time.

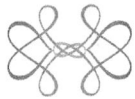

Raven's afternoons were spent in certain ladylike activities such as reading and needlework or correspondence. She'd already had two gossipy letters from Bri letting her in on all the recent Society *on dits*. She decided to return to her room and answer the most recent one she'd received.

She was just closing her door when it was suddenly pushed wide. She stared up into the hard brown eyes of Lord Greyden.

"What do you want?" she asked unnecessarily.

The young lord favored Raven with a malevolent look. "I know you are my brother's whore just as you were the whore for half the aristocracy. It is only fair that I have a sample of your wares."

She almost laughed. If only he knew exactly what his brother had gotten from her. She'd be only too pleased to show the annoying Greyden precisely what that was.

Raven allowed her dislike to show. "I will never allow you to touch me, Lord Greyden."

"It will be rape then? How entertaining," mused the young man with a sneer. "Tell me, Swan, is it possible to rape a whore?"

Raven saw his point. Unless someone cared enough to complain or interfere, it would not be rape. It happened all the time and even Raven wasn't sure that Tristan cared enough to interfere. Greyden was his brother after all.

She took a step back. She would NOT beg him to leave her be. She would, however, defend herself, the consequences be damned. Reaching behind her, she grasped the first object that came to hand. She was inwardly relieved it was a heavy silver candlestick and not something completely useless like her hairbrush.

Something in her manner must have given her away. Greyden suddenly leapt at her. Her struggle lasted only moments and she was quickly unarmed. He tossed the weapon away, retaining his hold on her.

Backing her slowly towards her bed, he snarled, "You have been a thorn in my side since the day I met you. It is time you learned your place."

"Considering how you loathe me, I am surprised you can find the inclination to bed me," she snapped back.

"I do not deny your beauty, Ebony Swan. No man with eyes could look upon you and not desire you. I object to your superiority."

With that, he gave an almighty push and sent her sprawling across the bed. He immediately followed her, pressing her down into the feather ticking.

Her look of surprise at his statement didn't seem to register. Had she really behaved towards him as if she were better than him?

She struggled to free her hands from behind her back. He was slightly preoccupied with tearing at the bodice of her gown. She managed to free her left hand and swung wildly at his head. She caught him on the ear and he howled in shock and pain but, unlike Tristan, he did not ease up on her. Instead, he grabbed her flailing arm with one hand and wrapped the other tightly around her throat. He squeezed until blackness welled up before her, threatening to take her under.

Desperately, she choked out, "Wife."

It was barely a whisper of sound but it succeeded in loosening his stranglehold. "What did you say?" he demanded.

"Your wife," she whispered around the pain in her throat. "Lily. What of Lily?"

He came off her suddenly, springing halfway across the vast room. He stared at her as if she was crazed. "What do you know of Lily?"

Raven sat up, gingerly rubbing her bruised throat. "I have met her, Lord Greyden. Several times, in fact. She is a sweet, unspoiled beauty who loves you very much. At the moment, I admit to having no idea why that is."

Apparently, neither did Greyden. He shook his head, bewildered. "Why…?"

Raven sighed and rose from the bed. "My lord, I would rather not say this considering you already think I believe in my own superiority but I feel it must be said. What you are doing to that girl is unconscionable. She loves you in spite of your obvious failings and you treat her as if she is lower than you are. It's not fair and you know she doesn't deserve it."

Several minutes passed as Raven stared at Greyden, her gaze unflinching. His eyes held a wealth of amazement, recognition, and surprisingly, hurt.

Then, to her dismay, his features hardened once again.

"Very clever, little harlot, but you will not escape me so easily."

Before Raven could react appropriately, Lord Greyden was on her. All she managed was an abbreviated scream, high and piercing but cut ruthlessly short by Greyden's hand on her throat.

She struggled valiantly, nearly panicked now. Her air was slowly diminishing and she could do nothing to relax his grasp on her slender throat. He seemed far stronger then his looks suggested.

And she couldn't deal him a blow such as she'd done to his brother. Her strength was fading. Finally, she slipped into a semi-unconscious state, limp as a ragdoll.

Oh, how she wished Tristan was there!

As if conjured, the door opened to crash into the wall, revealing the Duke of Windhaven.

Despite her desperate situation, Raven could not help but appreciate how melodramatic it all was.

Tristan, taking in the scene at a glance, was outraged. His own brother was...Dear God in heaven!

Moving faster than he'd ever moved before, the duke grasped his sibling by the hair and pulled him off Raven. Then he tossed him, like so much refuse, across the room. Greyden hit the wall so hard he was momentarily stunned.

Turning back to Raven, Tristan's heart stopped beating. He detected no movement in her slender body. Indeed, she seemed...dead.

"No," he whispered. Stepping closer, he stared hard at her. Then he saw it. Just the faintest rising of her chest.

He was beside her in the next instant, oblivious to the fact that his brother had slithered from the room.

"Rae, darling, breath," he instructed, gathering her close. He saw the bruises on her tender flesh and gritted his teeth in fury. Grey would pay dearly for his actions!

"Tris-tan."

It was nothing more than a croak and a faint one at that, but Tristan thanked God for small favors.

Raven slowly opened her eyes. She moved her head, trying to ease her neck, but her throat viciously protested even the slightest movement. She gasped.

"Don't move just yet, Rae. You are fairly beaten." He examined her throat carefully, muttering, "I'll kill him for this."

"No," she mouthed. "My fault. Don't. Family."

Having realized she was worried about his family and what it would do to them to discover a rapist numbered among them, he nodded reluctantly. Brother or no, his behavior was unacceptably criminal. But if it eased Raven's mind, he'd agree to anything.

"Did he…?"

"No."

From the state of her clothing, one couldn't have guessed how far his brother had gotten. Her skirts were rucked up to her thighs and her bodice was torn and Grey's clothing had been askew as well. But considering how he was strangling the girl, he could have been finished and tying up loose ends for all Tristan knew.

The fact that he hadn't actually raped her bought him a few more days of life, the duke decided.

Raven waved a hand in the air, indicating she wanted to rise. "No, you should lie down."

The look she bent on him told him what she thought of that idea and so he reluctantly helped her to a sitting position.

"Leave."

He frowned, hurt. "You want me to leave?"

She shook her head, then winced. She pointed at herself. He relaxed. "Oh, you want to leave." Then he scowled. "You want to leave?"

She rolled her eyes at him. With an all-encompassing wave of her right arm and a particularly violent jab at the bed she still sat upon, she left him in no doubt that it was the room she wanted to leave, not the estate.

He knew his relief was evident, as was her smile of understanding.

He acquiesced to her demand, politely offering to carry her. She laughed silently, indicating that his arm would be enough.

She stood, realizing far more bruising than she had at first supposed. Shakily, she smoothed her skirts down over her aching, bruised legs. Her bodice was irreparably damaged and she felt tears start.

It was shock, she knew. It was always a little time after such an incident that the shock set in. She felt her body start to tremble.

A strong arm came around her and in the back of her mind was panic. She fought it, knowing this was Tristan and he wouldn't hurt her. She moved stiffly into his embrace, willing control over her quaking body.

Ignoring her earlier assertion that she could walk, the duke swept her up into his arms, cradling her tight against his hard chest.

He took her to his own bedchamber. It was apparent she

wanted to keep the situation a secret and he knew no other place they could be undisturbed while she waited out the return of her voice.

Raven had no qualms about being with him in his room. Her desire to leave the scene of her near-rape had been so strong within her that she didn't really care where she ended up.

He sat down in a chair by the fire, settling her comfortably in his lap. Then he stroked her back until the trembles subsided and she rested calmly against him.

"Better?" he asked softly into her hair.

She smiled into his cravat and nodded her head. It wasn't so painful this time. Her voice should return presently.

"Would you like to talk about it?" he asked gently. She made no reply he could identify, so he added, "It must have been a frightening experience. The shock is great, or so I understand. I am surprised you have recovered as quickly as you have."

She looked up at him at that. Her eyes were wide, her poise restored.

Trying out her voice, she whispered, "You don't imagine this is the first time this has happened, do you?" Her voice was huskier than usual and faintly amused, in spite of the horrifying subject.

He gave her a look of utter disbelief. "This has happened before?"

She chuckled lightly, moving her fingers against her throat when the action caused a twinge of discomfort. "It has. I have dealt with more attempts than I can count, as have my…protectors."

"Good God, woman!" He would have said more, but indeed, what more was there to possibly say?

Pushing slightly away from him, she added, "One has never gotten as far as Greyden. I think that would explain the severity of my shock."

He just stared at her.

"Truly, Tris, I am fine now. It is nothing to dwell on."

He was amazed. How could she view rape as just another daily occurrence?

Of course, in the profession she'd chosen, he supposed it was nearly a daily occurrence. Gentlemen, after all, were not the only ones who would try to take a beautiful woman against her will.

Placing one hand tenderly against her cheek, he whispered, "I am sorry, Rae, for all you have had to endure in your life."

It was with a supreme effort that Raven avoided bursting into hysterical tears. One drop of moisture did manage to escape. Tristan leaned forward and kissed it away.

It was only natural, therefore, for him to proceed to her bruised throat and on down to her exposed breasts.

When she moaned, Tristan returned enough to himself to look at her closely. He saw something in her eyes that caused his breath to catch in his throat.

Her name came out in a breathless whisper as he took her mouth in a kiss that robbed them both of all sense.

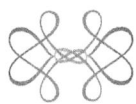

Chapter Twelve

Things should have gotten better from there. But they did not. Far from it, Raven was eaten by guilt at her loss of control and adversely blamed Tristan. Their encounters after that afternoon were spent snapping at each other over petty trifles.

To everyone else, it appeared as though they'd had a marital row, therefore, nothing to be concerned about. They conducted themselves well in public and that was all that mattered.

So it was with some annoyance that, after dinner one evening, Greyden suggested his dear sister-in-law favor them with a taste of her thespian skills, of which, he remarked with a smirk, he was sure she'd make a decent showing.

Tristan was tempted to murder his brother then and there. In his mind, it was Grey's fault he and Raven were at outs with each other. Had the mad clunch not tried to force himself on her, she would not have ended up in his arms sooner than she was actually ready.

Raven, seeing no way to politely demur when everyone seemed so enthusiastic about it, rose to her feet to comply with their demands.

"Have you a specific piece in mind?" she asked the room in general.

Without thinking, Tristan said, "Romeo and Juliet."

This suggestion was met with satisfaction on the parts of the aunts and even the dowager was gracious enough to incline her head in agreement.

Raven, knowing the play by heart, nevertheless requested Tristan's copy from the library. The duke gestured to the footman on duty who bowed and left.

A few moments had to be endured before the footman's return. Raven moved to where Tristan sat. Upon her approach, he rose to his feet.

"May I have a word with you?"

He moved a few feet away with her. "You really don't have to do this, Rae, if you would be uncomfortable," he assured her.

She smiled, almost laughing. "I could never find acting uncomfortable, my lord, even in these circumstances. I merely wonder at your choice."

"Call it a whim, if you like. I'd like to see you as Juliet again."

"And who shall play my Romeo?"

He hesitated, looking closely at her. She almost held her breath, waiting for his reply.

He shrugged, the ghost of a smile crossing his lips. "I will, who else?"

Relief mingled with dismay in Raven's breast. She had feared Greyden would be constrained to oblige the group with his participation. She had also feared Tristan might be.

What she feared most was the bittersweet thrill she felt at the thought of reciting any part of the tragic love story with Tristan. It was too close to the truth, she reflected morosely.

The footman returned, handing the requested playbook to his master. He then settled against the wall, ready should he be needed and secretly thrilled he would get to witness the actress at work.

Tristan and Raven took a few moments to confer over what scene they should read. When they couldn't agree— Raven wanted something mundane while Tristan wanted the same scene they had played in the library over a month ago—Freya suggested they simply open the book and recite whatever was on the page.

The key players shrugged. It was a solution. Tristan did the honors.

"Act II, scene 2," the duke said, privately pleased. Raven very nearly scowled at him. He scanned the page for a moment. "Let's start here," he said. "Line 107."

"Very well, my lord."

Tristan skimmed the lines then looked up. Gazing deep into her dark eyes, he recited, "'Lady, by yonder blessèd moon I swear / That tips with silver all these fruit-tree tops —'"

"'O, swear not by the moon, the inconstant moon, / That monthly changes in her circled orb, / Lest that thy love prove likewise variable.'"

Raven's response was automatic. She didn't even look at the book. Indeed, the words seemed to come from her, said as they were with such vehemence.

Tristan, distracted by her feeling, hesitated as he glanced very briefly at the book. "'What shall I swear by?'"

"'Do not swear at all,'" she said. She paused, a pensive look suffusing her features. "'Or, if thou wilt, —'" Suddenly, her expression cleared, changing into something altogether different—"'swear by thy gracious self, / Which is the god of my idolatry, / And I'll believe thee.'"

Tristan, a little dazed, didn't bother to look at the playbook, his gaze locked firmly on his companion's beautiful face. "'If my heart's dear love—'"

Raven waved a negligent hand. "'Well, do not swear: although I joy in thee, / I have no joy of this contràct tonight: / It is too rash, too unadvised, too sudden; / Too like the lightening, which doth cease to be / Ere one can say "It lightens."'" She paused infinitesimally, staring so hard at him that he felt the urge to fidget. "'Sweet good night! / This bud of love, by summer's ripening breath, / May prove a beauteous flower when next we meet. / Good night, good night! As sweet repose and rest / Come to thy heart as that within my breast!'" She moved, as if to leave.

"'O, wilt thou leave me so unsatisfied?'"

Color flared in Raven's cheeks. The duke's tone was not appropriate for mixed company. The look in his eyes was even less so.

In an unprecedented lapse of memory, Raven had to glance at the book for her next line—which brought her uncomfortably close to her partner.

Bending slightly over the book for no more than a moment was all the opportunity Tristan needed to breathe in her ear, "Will you, Rae? Leave me unsatisfied?"

She straightened, not bothering to move away from him. "'What satisfaction canst thou have tonight?'"

Tristan nearly choked at the innocence of her tone and expression. He made his own expression mirror hers. "'The exchange of thy love's faithful vow for mine.'"

"'I gave thee mine before thou didst request it: / And yet I would it were to give again.'"

The sincerity of her words drew Tristan up short. He delivered his next line with what their audience thought was a measure of the real bewilderment Romeo may have felt.

"'Wouldst thou withdraw it? For what purpose, love?'"

Raven smiled. "'But to be frank, and give it thee again. / And yet I wish but for the thing I have: / My bounty is as boundless as the sea, / My love as deep; the more I give to thee, / The more I have, for both are infinite.'"

She stopped, her voice having dropped to a nearly inaudible whisper, an arrested expression stealing over her beautiful face.

Tristan closed the book. Raven stared up at him, horrified. She recalled her conversation with Bri three weeks ago. The other woman had claimed Raven was in love with the duke. She had told herself then that Bri was seeing romance where none existed.

Now, Raven realized the awful truth: she had fallen irrevocably in love with the Duke of Windhaven. However could she go on with a normal life after this?

And the duke, seeing her expression, wondered just what was passing through that agile little brain of hers. She seemed almost...repulsed.

The room suddenly erupted into applause. The two players came back to the present, smiling automatically at the accolades they received.

Raven still looked pale, drawn. Tristan watched her closely, worried over her odd behavior.

With a final smile, Raven pleaded fatigue and begged to be excused. Tristan offered to escort her up, an offer she adamantly declined.

"I will be fine, my lord, truly. Please do not leave on my account," she added calmly.

He acquiesced, reluctantly, allowing her to leave the room. As she moved through the open door, held by the ever-attentive footman, Grey said, "How fabulous, Tris. If one didn't know better, one would think your wife has tread the boards in her lifetime."

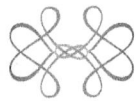

Tristan stood at the window of his study, staring down at the lake. Raven was there again, sitting on the bank. Her hair was pinned up, as usual since she had arrived there, a few dark tendrils escaping to blow in the sporadic breeze.

He sighed deeply. The woman haunted him. His days were spent in business but thoughts of her would creep in to distract him.

And his nights…dear God, he didn't think he'd had a decent night's sleep since she'd seduced him in his room five days ago.

Visions of that afternoon danced in his head, tantalizing him. He felt his body react and was tempted to order her brought to him like a medieval lord demanding his rights.

Disgusted, he turned away from the window. He was going insane. His desire for her was elemental but went far deeper. He wanted all of her, her heart most of all.

Shoving a hand through his already disordered locks, he

nearly growled in frustration.

Lately, he was at a loss how to go about winning her heart. The blasted woman acted as though he had the plague. Or the pox.

Swinging back around, he looked down on her. She was no longer alone. Greyden was there, talking to her and from the look on her face, she was not enjoying the conversation.

Damn his brother anyway!

Servants stood quickly aside as the dignified Duke of Windhaven stormed from his home, murder in his eyes.

Lord Greyden Cramshaw never saw it coming. A fist seemed to fly out of nowhere, smashing into his face with bone-crushing force.

He went down like a ton of bricks. His brother, nobility personified, stood over him, breathing fire.

"Get up."

Raven, frozen in horror, moved quickly forward. "Tristan, stop. We were talking, simply talking. Nothing more."

The duke, still staring at his brother, asked, "Did he offer you insult?"

Raven hesitated, for Greyden had indeed insulted her. But no matter how much she felt the young lord deserved it, she couldn't condone the kind of violence the duke was determined to mete out. "Tristan, please, leave it be."

The duke looked away, gauging the lie in Raven's black eyes. She saw that he divined the truth in her expression.

"You promised, Tristan. You promised," she reminded him desperately.

Neither of them was paying any attention to Greyden. He lay, seemingly insensible until Tristan turned away. Then, moving stealthily, he regained his feet.

He'd swung at his brother's head before Raven could call out a warning. Tristan stumbled to the side, shaking away the dizziness in his head.

With a growl of feral rage, he charged his brother. They collided, went staggering onto the half-frozen lake.

Raven's heart stopped. The men were so enraged they didn't feel the telltale shiver of cracking ice.

Tristan wrestled his brother into a stranglehold, squeezing until the younger man went into a frenzy, clawing desperately at the duke's arms.

Suddenly, Greyden slumped, unconscious. Tristan released him, his breath coming in short gasps as his lungs tried to draw in chilled February air.

Then, he blinked. Grey was gone. The duke had only a split second to draw in a great gulp of air before the icy water closed over his head.

Never in her life had Raven screamed as she did in that moment.

Chapter Thirteen

Weary, discouraged, and just plain depressed, Raven slumped in a chair by the duke's bed as his body was again wracked with shivers. She drew yet another blanket over him, wondering what else she could possibly do.

They had already tried everything. Nothing seemed to be working. He still shook, muttered incoherently, and tried to throw off his coverings. If Raven hadn't known better, she'd have thought he was feverish.

But he wasn't. His body was cool to the touch but not alarmingly so. He should have been back on his feet by now, nearly a day later.

Crossing to the window, Raven stared out as pale streaks of dawn lit the early morning sky. She folded her arms in front of her, hugging herself and the chill she felt deep inside.

What was she to do? In the back of her mind was a remedy she was sure would work for Tristan, but her own sense of self-preservation prevented her from doing it.

But she loved him. Wasn't her own life worth that of his?

With a decisive nod, Raven moved to lock all the bedroom doors. If Tristan was anywhere near his right mind, she knew where her next actions would lead.

She quickly shed all her clothes until she was naked. Then, climbing onto the high bed, she snuggled under the covers with him.

He stilled, the only movement in his large frame the shaking he could not control. As if sensing what she was doing, he turned towards her, opening his green eyes to stare at her blankly.

"Rae?"

The former actress sighed. It was no use, really. She'd do anything for this man.

Moving so she was flush against him, Raven kissed him softly on the lips. "You are so cold, my love."

Her husky voice was soothing, calming. She reached around him, smoothing her clever fingers up over his shoulders and down his back almost to his buttocks. She continued this motion until his shivers subsided, then disappeared completely.

It had been panic, as she'd suspected. The cold had dissipated several hours before; it was the fear that had held him captive.

Tristan's arms moved to hold her close, nothing more. He shivered one last time, a great wracking shudder that communicated his fear into his slender companion. She shivered with him, nearly overcome with the extent of what he'd been through.

"Grey?"

Raven frowned. "He is alive," she said. She hesitated, wanting very much to avoid telling him the rest. "But he will not be the same, Tristan. Something happened in the water. He struck his head or was under too long. We're not sure. The doctor is on his way but…"

The duke shuddered again, a tear slipping down his face to soak Raven's dark hair.

Placing her lips against his collarbone, she whispered, "Tell me about it, Tristan. Please."

He didn't want to talk about it. It was too shameful a secret to reveal. His family didn't even know how he loathed that lake. And now, he had the added burden of his brother's injury on his conscience.

Shaking his head in denial, Tristan drew her body up far enough to reach her lips, kissing her deeply until she pressed into him, seeking greater contact.

But then she pulled away. "Please, Tris. You need to talk about this."

He glared at her. "I don't want to." His voice sounded petulant, like a spoiled child.

She smiled affectionately. "I know you don't, dearest, but you have spent nearly a day shaking with chills. You are not feverish, you are not even cold anymore. Please talk to me."

He grimaced. "How can you ask me to talk when you are so wantonly plastered against me?" He moved his lower body just enough to make her catch her breath. His expression turned decidedly wicked. "Isn't there something you'd much rather do with me, my pet?"

She laughed a trifle breathlessly. "You know there is." A look of extreme concern settled on her beautiful countenance. "Please, my love."

He smoothed the fingers of his free hand into her midnight tresses, drawing them away from her face. "I cannot tell you no," he murmured, "when you call me that. But you know that, do you not?"

She said nothing, merely waited for him to speak.

"I tell you this under protest."

She nodded, smiling tenderly.

With a weary sigh, he closed his eyes and confessed, "I fell in the lake as a child." At her lack of reaction, he glanced down at her. "Shocking, I know," he muttered dryly.

"It was winter, I was five." He received a gasp at that. "Yes, damn cold time to go for a swim. I was in the water for five minutes before my mother was able to get me out."

Despite the horror of such a thing happening to such a young child, Raven sensed it was not the reason for his gut-wrenching terror.

It wasn't. "Somehow, I survived. My mother, who'd never been in the best of health, died three weeks later. My father never let me forget it was my fault and I should have died instead of her."

Raven bit her lip to stifle her distress. "Oh, my dear, how awful for you." A new thought occurred to her. "But if you were five, Greyden and Freya aren't your..."

"Oh, they are," he confirmed. "Father remarried an heiress one season, barely out of the schoolroom, got two children on her and promptly killed himself in a hunting accident. I was eighteen when he 'shuffled off this mortal coil.' Freya was a babe in arms, her mother ill-equipped for life as the Marchioness of Hastings. The fool woman took her own life a month later."

He paused, willing back the automatic panic he felt when the series of events were brought to mind. "And it was all my fault," he finished in a dead voice.

Raven's body jerked. She moved his head around to face her. Her angry look was not lost on him and he wondered if she, too, would tell him what a worthless human being he was.

"You were a child, Tristan. It was not your fault and your father should be shot for making you feel that way."

His eyes widened with each word that left her mouth. "I was five, Rae, not two. I was fully aware that I was doing something I shouldn't."

She shook her head. "No, you were but a child. You did not know your mother would risk her life should something happen to you. She should have alerted one of the footmen to rescue you, one of the grooms, somebody who was better equipped to do so. She should have—"

He kissed her. Tears coursed down her cheeks, mingling with their kiss.

She was silent when the duke finally pulled back. A watery chuckle emerged then. "That was effective, was it not?"

He didn't bother to reply. He kissed her again, pouring his heart and soul into the kiss, his gratitude, love, and longing. He gave her everything he had, everything he was, and everything he would ever be.

"No more talk. Let me love you."

The words were nothing more than a breath against her lips, but Raven felt the entreaty to the depths of her heart and soul.

Refusing to examine the consequences, she smiled, inviting his touch in the most elemental way she knew how.

She kissed him.

Much later that morning found Raven walking towards

the lake.

She felt drawn to the frozen body of water. It played such a large part in her love's history, she couldn't help but be entranced by it.

And it was here that she realized he loved her.

He had fought his own brother, been enraged by the thought that he may have dared insult her.

Sitting as still as stone, Raven watched the absence of life. It was amazing to her, to see what appeared a lifeless piece of landscape. But beneath the surface, below the ice, the water positively teemed with life, even now, in the freezing cold of winter.

She sat there contemplating nature for hours. The cold finally began to penetrate her outer garments, making her shiver.

Which served to remind her of the events of that morning, just after dawn's pale streaks suffused the night sky. Tristan had controlled their encounter, skillfully taking her beyond heaven with his clever hands and mouth.

She should feel guilt, as she had after every other union in which she'd participated.

And she did, she thought with a sigh. It was wrong. They were not married despite the world's belief to the contrary.

She should be married. She wanted to be married. Marriage was always a dream of hers. But after her life in the theater, that was all it was, a dream. So she had taken what little happiness she could, first with Adam, then with Levi, and now...

Now she had Tristan, the Duke of Windhaven, in her bed and unfortunately, firmly implanted in her heart.

The only problem was...she wasn't happy.

She was miserable. She had been raised in a strictly moral household. Her father and mother had instilled a sense of upright morality in their daughters that was a little out of place in the social echelon in which she'd grown up. In fact, it was a little out of place in any echelon of the world as she knew it.

It was, therefore, a very difficult decision that led her to the theater for work. She knew she was endangering her future when she signed on as a lesser character in the Theatre Royal's adaptation of Shakespeare's *As You Like It*. At the time, it seemed her only option.

She'd had no illusions then of her talent. She had no false modesty; she was good and she knew it. She also knew she had the kind of talent that could get her by without having to fall back on the age-old true profession of actresses.

Then Adam had come along, radiating virility and masculine appeal and she'd felt lust for the first time. And she'd been powerless to hold on to her closely guarded virtue.

When he ended their liaison, she'd felt her world shift just a little. But she was the Ebony Swan, renowned for her poise and devotion to the stage. She had had no time for heartbreak.

But Levi, Lord Greville, had proven far more addictive than she'd suspected. Her base desires had taken over again, accepting his offer of protection.

Raven shuddered at her memories of the dark months after Levi had let her go. She had become so obsessed with him that her head was not in control when she'd approached Aurora Glendenning, intent on mischief.

Deadly mischief.

A single tear slipped down her pale, chilled skin. The worst to happen in that situation was Levi's willing forgiveness and Aurora's offer of friendship.

Biting her lip, Raven firmly held back the sob threatening to escape. It was hard reliving the past, but in light of her newest dilemma, she thought it might be best to remind herself just why she could not go on in this way.

"Rae?"

It was fatalistic sigh that escaped then, followed by a choked sob. Tristan sat down next to her, drawing her into the circle of his arms.

"Whatever is the matter?" he asked, his voice gruff with concern.

She shook her head, as yet unable to speak.

So he just held her silently. Raven finally managed to stem the tears and looked up at him.

"What brings you to the lake?"

He shuddered imperceptibly. "Inner demons," he admitted, "and a dark siren. What brings you out here?"

Raven shivered, feeling the cold of several stationary hours. "The same," she murmured. He eased his cloak open, pulling the edges around them both in a little cocoon of warmth.

Leaning back against his chest, she asked, "Do you think I'll ever learn to bury my conscience so deep it never bothers to alert me to my misdeeds?"

His frown was apparent in his voice. "Why would you want to?"

"Because I want to be with you."

He stopped breathing. "And your conscience objects to that?"

She didn't reply. She just stared off into the distance, soaking up the warmth of his body, wishing for what could never be.

"Rae?"

"I have never told you of my childhood, have I?"

"No."

"Would you like to know a few things about me, my lord?"

His reply was instantaneous. "Of course."

She laughed lowly. "You may regret your eagerness when you learn a few of my secrets."

He drew a breath. "You don't have to tell me anything you don't want to, Raven. I admit I'd like to know everything there is to know about you but I'll not pressure you."

She turned her head to look up at him, a smile twisting her full lips. "How very magnanimous of you, Tristan Cramshaw." A feather light kiss followed these words. Then she turned her face away.

"It is only fair, I think, to tell you. I forced you, after all, to exorcise your own personal demons."

Settling herself more comfortably in his arms, she began with her earliest memories. He listened, fascinated, at this inner glimpse of the woman he loved.

After a moment, he began to frown. He interrupted her recitation. "Do you realize, pet, that your early childhood is alarmingly absent of memories?"

"What do you mean?"

"Well, think back to the very first thing you remember. How old were you?"

"Honestly, I think was three. I remember this orange kitten that my father gave me…" Her voice trailed off, a perplexed frown marring her brow. Speaking slowly, thinking the memory out as she gave it voice, she said, "The kitten was Monsieur Boots. He had four white paws. He was given to me on my fifth birthday. The funny thing was, my father wouldn't let me keep him."

She twisted around again to look at him. "Why would he give me a gift and then not let me keep it?"

Tristan had no answer to that. It was odd to say the least.

"You were five?" he asked, catching the hidden detail in her tale.

She started. "I suppose I was. I had thought I was younger." She shrugged, frowning. "Father gave me a locket, too, but I lost it."

Tristan sensed the pain in this admission. "What else do you remember?"

Her brow furrowed. "A boy." Her eyes shot wide. "Why would I remember a boy?"

He shook his head, as baffled as her. "Did you have a brother?"

"No..."

"...But...?"

"He was a beautiful boy, darkly fine. Black unruly hair and black eyes. We were very close. I wonder who he was?"

"Rae, none of this makes sense."

Raven grimaced. "You don't have to tell me. I know."

Shaking herself out of her confusion, she continued where she'd previously left off.

It soon came to light the reason behind her odd question about her conscience. Tristan was amazed to learn a former actress had been raised in a Methodist-like home. The only difference seemed to be that her parents were not as straight-laced as most. They allowed gaiety and fun; they simply stressed the importance of chastity. It was actually something he could admire.

She told him her choice in acting was not made lightly. She had realized then the enormity of her decision but she was determined to remain chaste in honor of her parents' memories if for no other reason.

"It was," she admitted, "my unfortunate appreciation for the male form that truly brought me low. Adam was determined to have me and I was equally determined to resist. But it was all for naught." She stopped, the pain too much to bear.

"Never mind all that," Tristan told her bracingly, part of him so desperate to avoid this particular subject he would grasp at straws. "Why do you still feel guilty for your past encounters?"

She gave him a look that bordered on incredulity. "It is not those encounters so much as the most recent ones that bother me, my lord. Not to mention the ones yet to occur."

His heartbeat picked up a beat at her salient admission. Then it stopped altogether. She felt guilty about them. She was miserable because they'd been together.

But why...?

It struck him like a bolt of lightning. Because they were not married. He, in his overweening pride and conceit, had somehow forgotten that the legalities of their union were in question. It was clear to her that they were not married; he was beginning to have doubts about everything. Her reciting of her memories were odd, to say the least.

He squeezed her a little tighter. "I'm sorry, Rae. I didn't

realize."

It wasn't difficult to determine what he was talking about. She had watched his face the last few moments, marveling at how revealing his features could be.

But at the heartfelt apology in his face and eyes, she thought she might break down and cry again.

Fighting for sanity, she told him, "None of it is your fault. I am to blame. It is my wantonness and lack of self-control, my lord, that—"

"Nonsense," he interrupted briskly. Suddenly feeling chilled, as he should having sat in the cold as long as they had, the duke stood, bringing Raven to her feet as well.

"We must return to the house, my dear. It is nearly time for luncheon and I am famished."

Raven stared a little strangely at him. "I have not finished with my confession."

A smile threatened. "I am not a priest, Raven. You have no call to confess to me."

"My lord, Tristan, please. There are things I must tell you."

He sighed. "Very well. Join me in the library. We can be reasonably private there without the threat of our base urges taking advantage."

"Thank you," she replied sincerely.

Chapter Fourteen

The library, vast chamber that it was, had an eerie haunting quality to it. Raven reveled in it, matching her mood so well as it did.

The duke led her to a far table, seating her with aplomb nearest the crackling fire. With a bow, he disappeared into a room at the back, only to reappear moments later with Mr. Muffton in tow.

"Muff will send a maid for our lunch, if you don't mind eating here."

She acquiesced with relief. Somehow, she felt at ease, calm, at peace within these book-lined walls. Her smile was sincerely pleased.

"Do you mind if I peruse the shelves while we wait?"

He agreed, going so far as to offer his arm. "Allow me to show you areas that may be of interest to you."

She gave a mock groan. "Please, no plays, my lord, I beseech you. I have had enough of acting for the nonce."

He chuckled. "Indeed no, my love. I have something far more...ladylike to interest you."

Thoroughly intrigued, she followed him to a shelf near the middle of the north-facing wall. He pulled a slim volume from a shelf, handing it to her with a flourish.

Taking it, Raven glanced at the title. "The Romance of the Forest," she said, laughing. "Could you not have picked something less prosy and more realistic?" she asked. Her face was aglow with amusement.

He caught his breath. His own mouth tilted up, mirroring her expression. "I admit the supposition that you would react thusly influenced my choice. However, you may be interested more in this."

So saying, he handed her another tome, thicker, bound in calfskin. Raven saw the title and glanced up at him in awe. "Ivanhoe? Do you have publishers send you books as they become available, then?"

He shook his head. "Open it."

Inside was an inscription. Windhaven, here is the latest. Enjoy. Scott.

She grinned at him. "Walter Scott is a personal friend of yours, is he? How...surprising."

He laughed. "Not really, I assure you. And I heard a

little rumor that our new king will be honoring Scott with a baronetcy."

"Oh, how wonderful," Raven said with some feeling.

They returned to their seats, Raven studying the book as if it were the holy grail. Tristan smiled to have pleased her in so simple a matter.

The servant entered presently with their repast.

Watching his lovely companion set the book aside with obvious reluctance, the duke couldn't help but laugh.

"You are fond of Scott, then?"

Raven smiled. "I admit I am. Next to Shakespeare, I think Mr. Scott may be the best storyteller to ever live."

"I'll be sure to pass on your compliment," the duke told her solemnly, going on to ruin the effect with a very un-dukely chortle.

This, Raven thought suddenly, this was what she wanted. This ease with the man she loved. Only…she wanted the permanence of marriage to go along with the ease.

Catching her melancholy expression, Tristan said soothingly, "Perhaps it is time you unburden yourself, my dear." At her uncertain look, he added, "As you can see, it helps."

He was right, she realized. He did seem more at peace within himself. He had even sat with her at the lake's edge, a place she knew he loathed quite fiercely.

"Very well." Taking a deep drink of her wine to fortify

herself, she said, "I may as well tell you the worst of it. My latest protector, an affair that ended some two years ago, met and married a wonderful girl of superb golden beauty and immense riches. I tried to discredit her, ruin her, and prayed for her demise, determined to help her along if the need arose."

"Help her along?"

"I withheld a critical piece of information that almost killed her. It certainly did destroy her peace of mind. In the process—and this is the worst of my sins—my selfish actions nearly cost a little girl her life. A child who had done nothing to deserve the fright she received when her own blood father held her for ransom."

"Did you know that he would do something so heinous?"

"Of course not. I did not claim an acquaintance with the man. But gossip did tell me that he was an acquaintance of hers. And instinct told me he was dangerous."

He waited for her to continue. She didn't. She just sat there, staring into her wine, awaiting his judgment.

Then she tilted her head up and back slightly. "It was quite the stupidest thing I have ever done, to be sure. I can only conclude I am sick, mentally unstable. I was so eaten up with jealousy I saw no other way to appease my desire for…ease."

Tristan reached out and took her hand. "You were upset, Rae. I'm sure you didn't mean her any real harm."

A spurt of laughter escaped her compressed lips. It had a hysterical quality to it. "Do you think, my lord? I wish I could be so sure. I had nothing but hatred for Aurora. And do you know what? She offered me friendship. Friendship when I wanted her dead."

"Rae…"

"That's not the worst of it, Tristan, not really. I realized it wasn't Aurora or Levi I hated. It was me. I hated me, the me I'd allowed myself to become. I was just another whore actress who couldn't keep her skirts down."

"Rae—"

She speared him with a look, the will not to cry drawing gasping little breaths from her throat. "A whore, my lord duke. Which is the sole reason you found it so easy to hire me for your insidious little charade."

Clamping her lips shut, she bit her lower lip hard enough to draw blood. Determinedly chanting the mantra she'd used since she was a child, Raven eased her mind and body back into that calm, composed place, the glue that held the frayed threads of her life together.

Tristan watched this transformation with some awe. He'd always wondered at her ability to seem utterly unaffected by mind-numbing events and crises. Now, watching her lips move silently, he saw that her poise was a mere shield. She felt chaotic at times; she had simply devised a way to control her urge to scream at life in general.

Except when he was the one in danger. He had heard her screaming fit to wake the dead when he fell through the ice. Her poise had completely deserted her then.

Opening her eyes suddenly, she said quietly, "It was after I came to my senses, so to speak, that I realized what I had almost done. It was then that I did this," She pointed at her wrist.

Tristan leaned forward, gazing at the slender appendage she held out to him. An ugly, faded scar ran the length of her wrist, a few smaller scars slashing across it. It was with a sick feeling in his stomach that he realized where it had come from.

He glanced up at her calm, composed features. There was a flicker of something in her eyes, a waiting expression that caught him in the middle, robbing him of words and breath.

She expected him to condemn her.

He stood, drawing her up with him. Placing his lips gently to the scarred flesh of her wrist, he murmured, "You poor dear girl. What were you thinking?"

There was enough concern and exasperation in his tone to snap her out of a little of her poise.

She jerked her hand away. "I was thinking I deserved to die. What does one usually think when they try to take their own life?"

He smiled, albeit a trifle woodenly. "Indeed."

The door was thrown open then to admit a flustered

footman, gasping for breath.

"Your grace! Guests arrive."

Sensing more was being said than was…well, being said, the duke snapped, "Who, man?"

"Preston, your grace. Lord Preston comes."

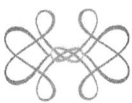

The Marquis of Preston stood at the mantle, staring down into the fire. His wife, Delilah, was sitting with seeming complaisance on the settee, hands primly folded in her lap.

He knew the gesture had nothing to do with how she actually felt. She was worried about the duke and Griffin, Lord Preston, knew it.

To be honest, he was worried as well. Anytime a man entered matrimony in a hole-in-the-wall fashion, friends ought to worry.

And Tristan had ever been a happy bachelor. Griff and his wife wondered what sort of woman had managed to sink her claws into the rich duke.

Hearing the door and his wife's muted gasp, he turned, dreading what he would see.

His pale brows rose, astonished. Tris stood with quite the most striking woman, darkly beautiful, finely drawn, fathomless black eyes, and a figure to rival a goddess.

But she looked vaguely familiar. He couldn't quite place her.

Delilah gasped again; Griff glanced at his wife to a see a look of shocked revulsion. Looking back at Tristan's companion, he narrowed his eyes.

Smiling, he strode forward, "The new Lady Windhaven, I presume. Lord Preston, at your service." Damn, she was even lovelier up close.

"My wife, Delilah."

The two women barely acknowledged the introduction. They stared at each other, sensing right away that they were not to be friends.

Lady Preston had recognized the Ebony Swan and was indignant that her husband's friend had been so taken in. Did he actually believe the woman was something she was not?

Griff shook his friend's hand, noting the wooden expression on the duke's face. He wasn't, therefore, surprised when the duke finally spoke.

"What are you doing here, Griff?"

The marquis shrugged, smiling. "We heard you had married. It behooved us to discover what sort of girl could bring you up to scratch."

Lady Preston added, "Yes, dear Tristan. Just what…sort of girl did win your title and fortune?"

The barb was not subtle and Raven smiled with a marked amount of contempt. "Wouldn't you like to know," she murmured.

Tristan squeezed Raven's hand in warning. "As she

stands before you, Del, I can't have heard you correctly, I think. Would you like to rephrase your question?"

Delilah stepped forward as though to do Tristan an injury. Her husband took her arm in what was supposed to appear an affectionate hold but actually restrained her impetuosity.

"Do you stay?" the duke asked then, indicating they should be seated. He moved to another settee and firmly pulled Raven down beside him. He retained his hold on her hand, lacing their fingers together.

Raven wore her best Swan expression, poised, perfectly serene. She showed not the faintest unease before Tristan's disapproving friends.

The marquis and marchioness sat across from them, watching them both closely. Delilah reached up to adjust her hair, whispering behind her arm, "She's an actress, Griff. Ebony Swan. Juliet."

Griff's eyes grew large. He focused his gaze on Raven's face, picturing long, straight black locks flowing free and impassioned tears of heartbreak over the still body of her love.

Raven smiled radiantly at him. Leaning a little to the side, she told Tristan in a stage whisper, "Methinks he doth know me."

Delilah released an outraged yelp at the words, confirming as they did the fact that they sat in the same room as an actress. Griffin again took his wife's arm, keeping her firmly at his side.

"Care to explain, my friend?"

Tristan snorted. "No."

"Darling, you can't leave them in suspense like this," Raven remonstrated gently.

Tristan bit back the shout of laughter that threatened to emerge at her tone. With as straight a face as possible, he said, in a tone of cajoling sweetness, "But darling, it is really none of their business." Leaning closer, he kissed her lightly on the cheek.

"Oh, good God, he's bewitched!" exploded the marchioness in disgust.

Tristan dropped his hand, unable to hold back his laughter anymore. Raven joined him, although her amusement held a certain bitter quality that was hard to mask.

"And what, might I ask, did that accomplish?" asked Griff, visibly annoyed.

The duke shrugged, forcing his features into a polite social mask. "It really is none of your business, Griff."

"Well, I like that," Delilah muttered with some heat. "We come haring down here, worried unto death, and the stupid clunch hasn't even the wit realize how he's been duped."

Tristan stood. Or, he tried to, rather. Raven clutched his hand so tightly, he had no choice but to stay where he was, glaring daggers at his best friend's wife.

"Lady Preston, to what are you alluding?"

Raven had never heard Tristan speak like that. His tone was hard, with an underlying menace that spoke of the possibility of imminent violence.

And that against a lady, no less!

Griffin, for once, made the decision to keep his bride quiet and answer the question himself. "Apparently, your... wife, is not Lady Rachael Eliot. She is an actress, Tris. I'm sorry."

Raven smiled. It was such a knowing smile that the Prestons sat back a little, disturbed by the expression. She should have been quaking in her little kid slippers to have been so found out.

Tristan rolled his eyes heavenward. "Grant me patience," he muttered to unseen beings. With a weary sigh, he said, "Griff, Del, believe it or not, she really is Lady Rachael." He ignored the warning pressure from his companion. "How you knew her before is past. Leave it be."

The couple across from them shared a confused glance. "Are you saying the daughter a peer tread the boards?" the marchioness asked with a measure of patent disbelief.

The duke shrugged one broad shoulder, leaning back in apparent unconcern. "Think what you wish. I have not the ability to control your beliefs." He rested his arm along the back of the settee, placing his hand on Raven's neck.

Raven tried very hard not to be distracted by the

massaging motions of his hand on her bare flesh.

Griffin stared at their interplay with a look of incredulity. Then, shaking his head slightly, he asked, "Tris, do you not trust us? I should think you would let us know what is going on as we are the oldest of friends."

Tristan met his friend's pale gray eyes. "You expect me to believe that, when the first thing you do upon arrival is insult the woman I love and then insult me by suggesting I know her not at all?"

Three faces looked at him in shock.

The Prestons, although a love match themselves, were astonished that Tristan's was as well. He was a duke, after all, with a profligate younger brother and a duty to the succession. He should have looked over this season's crop of *débutantes* and chosen the one most suited to be the Duchess of Windhaven, not an actress with the eyes and manner of a seductress.

Raven, for her part, though suspecting Tristan had certain feelings for her had not heard them voiced before and was dazed by the feeling of euphoria that quickly rose in her breast. Had they been alone, she would not have been able to stop herself from dragging him to the nearest bed. Hell, she would have settled for the settee on which they sat.

And Tristan, not yet having realized exactly what little tidbit he'd let fall, looked at them all as if they were the ones ready for Bedlam.

Then he caught the look of unbridled hunger in Raven's eyes and felt himself react instantly. He realized then what he had let slip. He suddenly wished their guests would make themselves scarce so he could show Raven just how much he loved her.

Hard on that thought he inwardly groaned. That wasn't going to happen again until they were properly married, he reminded himself. He didn't want to cause her anymore grief than she'd already had. If it bothered her to indulge, they wouldn't.

To that end, he dropped his hand away from her tantalizing flesh and his eyes away from her heated look... and saw his best friend looking at him blankly.

Grinning widely, the duke asked, "How long do you visit?"

Griff shrugged, glancing uncertainly at his wife. "A few days, at least, if you don't mind."

"Not in the least. Mrs. Benson will show you to your rooms."

The four occupants of the drawing room rose as one. Before any of them could move further, however, there was a scratching on the door, followed by the butler, announcing in stentorian tones:

"Sir Adam Prestwich, Miss Linnet Emerson."

"Oh, this is rich," murmured Delilah in disgust, knowing full well exactly who Sir Adam was to Tristan's wife.

Sparing the Prestons barely a glance, Adam marched up

to Raven and Tristan, pulling Linnet by the hand.

"We have a problem," he announced without preamble. "Where can we talk?"

The duke gestured toward the footman, Will. "Take the Prestons to Mrs. Benson." Will bowed, obeying instantly.

Griff balked at being sent away like a recalcitrant child. "What is this about trouble?"

Finding his patience wearing quite thin, the duke said curtly, "I'll repeat what I said before, Griff, it is none of your business. I apologize for my rudeness but there it is." So saying, he firmly herded them out.

Griff stood on the other side, his face nearly touching the closed door.

"Well!" exploded the marchioness with heat.

"Well, indeed," murmured Griff thoughtfully. Glancing down at Delilah he asked, "What say you to an extended stay, my love? There is quite a mystery here, unless I miss my guess."

His wife could only shake her head in exasperation. Turning decisively, they made their way to their rooms.

"They're gone," Tristan announced, pulling his head away from the door. "And they're planning an extended stay." At the odd looks from his three companions, he shrugged. "What?"

Keeping a weather eye on the duke, Adam explained his

abrupt arrival.

"Dunston's son has been poking around, asking questions. Seems someone recalled seeing you in London."

Raven frowned. "Why have you brought Linnet?" she asked, drawing the girl close to her side.

The baronet shrugged. "She missed you." Casting the child an affectionate glance, he added, "Didn't you, pet?"

Linnet, overwhelmed by the august company in which she found herself, merely smiled in response.

Raven sent her former protector a look of distress. "Does she know?"

"Yes, Rae. She always did. You do not give the child enough credit."

Linnet looked up at her sister. "I'm sorry, Rae. I didn't give up until I found out where you'd gone and why. Adam says I'm a credit to him." The last was said with a huge grin.

"Indeed?"

They all turned to look at Tristan, who stood by the door still, his arms crossed over his chest. His look and tone suggested they had better start explaining a few things before he lost his temper completely.

Raven stepped forward. "Tristan, this is my sister, Linnet. Linnet, his grace, the Duke of Windhaven."

Linnet performed a credible curtsy, her mouth a round little "O" of awe. "Your grace," she murmured.

The duke bowed. "Your sister. Excellent. Welcome, my

dear. Now, Prestwich, what matter if Dunston's asking questions?"

"He's asking about Raven, not Rachael."

"That is interesting. What led him to Raven, do you think?"

"I would suspect a set of circumstances that place her family near the place Rachael disappeared nearly twenty-two years ago."

"Lady Rachael Elisabeth Eliot," Linnet inserted then. "Mama mentioned her once when she thought I wasn't listening. Said the marquess still hadn't given up his search for his daughter. Then she asked papa what they should do."

Everyone stared at her. "What?" Raven asked faintly, her head swimming with possibilities too farfetched to consider.

The young girl gave her audience a limpid look. "They often talked when I was there. I was so quiet I think they believed I was simple. They didn't know I was storing information for later."

"You would excel in blackmail, my girl," Adam told her dryly.

Linnet smiled as if just paid the greatest of compliments.

"Getting back to the matter at hand, Huntley received a mysterious message from someone claiming to know you personally, duke. This message intimated that you married someone posing as Lady Rachael Eliot."

"Who the devil would have sent such a message?" Tristan asked, truly puzzled.

"Lord Greyden?" suggested Adam.

"Never. He wanted the actress not the noblewoman. It would not have served his purposes to have her hanged as an impostor."

"Who else would claim such a standing with a duke?"

"Perhaps it was him," Linnet offered almost in a whisper, pointing to the closed door.

Tristan stared at her, wondering if the child was a lackwit. "Who? Preston?"

"No, that other man. The squirrelly one."

Adam was now looking at her odd, as well. Linnet rolled her eyes heavenward, as if greatly put out by the stupidity of men, and moved to the door. She swung it wide to reveal the man she was speaking of, crouched down with his ear to where the keyhole would have been.

"Muffton!"

Even Linnet jumped at the menacing tone of the duke's voice. He advanced on his librarian, intent on murder. Adam stopped him with a few well-chosen words.

"Huntley's been dispatched here to investigate further, so killing the weasel now will do no good. And you," he added, addressing Muffton, "will pack your things and leave just as soon as may be. You will walk to Lower Kempworth and take the stage to whatever stop is farthest from here. You will then take another stage and do the same. Repeat the process once more and there you will stay. And do not think that I will not know if you do not do exactly as I have instructed. If I find that you have ignored my orders, I will find you and tell Windhaven where you are." He let the inherent threat sink in. "Now, go!"

The duke watched grimly as the little man scurried from the room with his tail between his legs. He then turned to his hitherto unwelcome guest and asked sweetly, "When did I hire you to speak for me?"

The youngest of their group drew their attention back to the vital topic at hand. And just in time, too, as her hero was about to lay into the duke without mercy.

"If Lord Huntley sees you," Linnet explained to her still silent sister, "he may take you up on charges or support the claim. We are unsure which."

"He will support the claim," the duke said decisively. He took a deep breath to calm his anger. "The scandal would be astronomical should he not and the fact that Raven is, in actuality, Lady Rachael would make his having her arrested rather self-destructive."

Raven, hitherto a mute witness to talk that concerned her very survival, suddenly couldn't stand anymore. For the second time in her life, she fainted.

Chapter Fifteen

"You really mustn't make a habit of this, my love."

Raven smiled at the chiding tone, not bothering to open her eyes. "Have I survived, then?"

A low chuckle greeted her question. "Indeed you have."

A moment of tense silence ensued that so unnerved Raven that she finally opened her eyes to peek at the man to whom she'd given her heart.

He looked so serious that she was tempted to pretend another faint just to avoid a lot of tedious questions.

Deciding against that, she tried to sit up. "Come, darling, help me up. I need to be up for your questions, I think."

Tristan obliged her, saying, "It is you who should be

asking the questions."

Having settled herself comfortably on the low chaise, she replied, "Indeed. What did you mean telling them I am Lady Rachael? You know it cannot be true."

"But it is. There are a few missing pieces of the puzzle, to be sure, but I have no doubt you are indeed Lady Rachael."

Her mouth dropped open. "But I cannot be, Tristan. I remember my parents quite clearly. And they loved me. I am not Lady Rachael."

Tristan stood and paced a few steps away from her. "Think, my dear. Just this morning you told me of certain memories that do not coincide with your upbringing. A cat your father gave you but said you couldn't keep. A dark-haired boy who was your best friend and constant companion. A locket given to you on your fifth birthday that you lost." He paused. "Well, I suppose that could have been Emerson." Shaking his head, he continued. "How do you explain any of this unless you are, indeed, someone else?"

Raven shrugged helplessly. "I cannot. But I also cannot believe I am the daughter of a peer. Do you realize what I've done?"

"Done?"

"Oh, Tristan. I was an actress. The daughter of a marquess simply does not do that. The daughter of a marquess would die before she would do something so damaging to her reputation, not to mention the fact that I have taken protectors. Dear Lord, Tristan, even if I am Lady Rachael, Dunston would never acknowledge me. In fact, he would have to have me arrested as an impostor to save his family the shame of an immoral woman in their family."

"Of all the nonsensical things I have ever heard!"

Raven's seldom seen temper ignited. "Nonsensical? It is my neck we are discussing here, your grace, not the cut of your coat. I can assure you I find nothing I've said to be nonsensical!"

"You are my wife. He wouldn't dare—"

"I AM NOT YOUR WIFE!"

They stared at each other in shock. Raven covered her mouth with her hand, astounded that such loud and angry words had come from her lips.

Tristan's face went blank in the face of her indignation. "A situation that will be remedied, Rae," he said softly.

In her frustration, Raven's eyes filled with tears. "No, Tristan, no. Dear God, can you imagine? A duke marrying an actress? You would be treated as a social pariah, scorned, pitied. If you need proof, just look to your friends. They were only too willing to believe you'd been duped." A tear escaped, winding slowly down her pale cheek. "I couldn't do that to you, my dear. I just couldn't," she whispered miserably.

The duke went to his knees before her. Gently brushing

the tear away, he asked, "Do you love me?"

She nodded, beyond the desire to keep any of herself from him. "I do. To my shame, I do."

"Then marry me, Rae. If you love me truly, marry me."

Another tear trickled from her dark eyes. "I love you"—he smiled—"too much to do that to you."

"I cannot live without you, Rae. My life was meaningless before I met you. I've loved you from the first moment I saw you. You cannot possibly love me if you mean to leave me in this agony I've lived in for thirty years."

The former actress released an exasperated sigh. "How can you love me, knowing what I am?" she asked. "Knowing I have had other men before you? Knowing how I compromised my own beliefs for a few minutes of sexual gratification? Knowing I am a whore?"

Her voice had risen to a near shout, her anxiety reaching out to him, causing his own temper to rise. Stepping back physically, he fisted his hands at his sides, straining against the urge to yell out his own anger. He realized a shouting match would get them nowhere.

Quietly, his voice heavy with feeling, he spoke. "What do I have to do to prove to you that I don't care what the devil anyone thinks?"

"And what they think of me? Will you beat everyone who casts their eyes towards me with either repugnance or licentiousness? Will you abuse those ladies who draw their skirts away and cross as far from me as possible to avoid the possible contamination of my presence?" She sighed deeply, her hand going to him in an appeal for understanding. "It would eat you alive, Tristan. And I would be at fault. I can't let that happen."

It was time to bow out gracefully, the duke realized. As long as she believed herself to be nothing more than an actress-turned-impostor, she would not be swayed.

He would simply have to wait until Dunston arrived and convince the man to accept Raven as his daughter...or else.

Adam stayed. He said Linnet needed to be with her sister and he wanted to be there in case things should go wrong.

Tristan didn't need to ask how things could go wrong. Should Dunston declare Raven an impostor and demand her immediate incarceration, Adam would get the actress safely away.

And so they believed themselves to be reasonably ready for the arrival of the man Tristan fully suspected of being Raven's brother.

It was therefore, rather a surprise when not only the Earl of Huntley but Lord Dunston himself presented themselves one afternoon two days after Adam's arrival. And with them they brought another gentleman, a man with a particular interest in the entire situation.

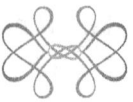

Raven had been crossing the hall when she heard the front bell ring. Will answered, a certain trepidation in his manner that Raven couldn't help but wonder at when he saw who it was.

"Kindly inform Lord Windhaven of our arrival."

Raven, who had been about to make her presence known, abruptly stilled. That voice. She knew that voice. But from where?

Needing to see the face of the man with that gravelly voice, she stepped closer.

She had only taken a few steps when the youngest of the three gentlemen suddenly turned, spearing her with a look. His eyes were black, fathomless, a flawless match to his dark, unruly locks. His features were finely drawn, classically beautiful. In fact, he looked just like...

"Rachael."

She started. The name was a mere breath of sound, hardly audible and yet she heard it clear to her marrow.

The young man moved forward but was stalled by the older gentleman's hand on his arm.

"Softly, Gervase. We do not know yet that it is she," this man cautioned.

Gervase. Gerry.

Raven gasped. "Gerry."

"See, Antoine, it is she. She knows me."

Antoine scoffed. "She heard me call you Gervase. Of course she would assume you went by Gerry in your youth. This is a skilled actress we are dealing with here."

Raven hardly heard them. She was in shock.

Benson, faithful servant that he was, sought to draw their collective attention back to himself. "My lords, if you would care to follow me, I will announce you."

They reluctantly did so, the oldest of the three strangely silent. He watched Raven like a hawk, noting every tiny movement of her hands, every indrawn breath, every tiny shudder that wracked her slender frame.

Moving with decision, he beckoned to her. "Come, my dear, as this is of concern to you. We shall have this out in no time and resolved to everyone's satisfaction. Come."

Raven stared at his outstretched hand. As if in a dream, she reached out and took his thin, bony fingers. He smiled charmingly and led her into the drawing room.

Tristan shocked family and servants alike when he ran through the manor and burst through the drawing room door as if Satan himself pursued him.

Raven stood at his entrance completely unprepared for the wild look of him. His green eyes swept the room, landed on her and he surged forward to pull her into his arms, hugging her close.

Stepping back a pace, he looked her over, his hands

framing her face. "Are you well?"

She released a startled laugh. "Of course I am well, my lord," she assured him softly. Gently moving his hands from her face, she added, "You are being disgracefully rude to our guests, my love."

Tristan became aware of the other occupants almost immediately. His grandmother was there as well as the aunts and Freya with Linnet perched beside her. Griff and Delilah sat with stunned looks on their faces and Adam was silently laughing at him from his stance before the fire. Greyden was noticeably absent due to his lingering injuries.

There were three new arrivals as well. Three gentlemen sat or stood to one side, conspicuous by their travel dress.

Bowing stiffly while retaining his hold on Raven's hand, he murmured, "Gentlemen, pray forgive me." His tone suggested he cared not one way or the other what they did.

Raven sent him an admonitory glance. "Tristan, this is my Lord Dunston, my Lord Huntley, and Comte du Larousse. Gentlemen, his grace, the Duke of Windhaven."

The dowager nodded graciously in Raven's direction, indicating her approval of the introductions. Raven smiled briefly at her, distracted by Tristan's reaction to these men.

After a terse acknowledgment of their identities, the duke rudely turned his back to their guests. "What has happened?" he demanded in a whisper. "Have they insulted you?"

A nervous laugh threatened. "They have hardly had

time, my lord. It has only been a few minutes, I promise, and the introductions took most of that. All is well, I assure you."

He breathed a sigh of relief. "Will had me believing they'd already hauled you away in chains." Glancing back at their rapt audience, he added, "Just who the devil is Comte du Larousse, anyway?"

Raven shrugged, saying nothing.

Adam approached, his look still revealing his amusement. "Are you going to ignore them all afternoon or ask a few questions?"

Tristan glared at the other man. "This is my house, I'll do what I damn well please. Apologies, Rae," he muttered automatically.

She snorted.

Adam threw a smile in her direction. "Does he remind you of anyone, Rae? A certain duke with an attitude problem, perhaps?"

With a genuine smile only slightly colored with bitterness, she said, "Derringer."

Tristan wasn't sure if he should be offended or thank them for the compliment. Derringer was a loose screw if ever there was one, but he was known for getting things done that no one else would dare attempt.

"That has nothing to do with anything. I think I made my point."

"Ah, but I think you miss the point, duke. That old man

over there holds Raven's life in his hands. Should he decide he doesn't want to acknowledge her, she will hang as an impostor."

Raven paled slightly at the words but said nothing.

Windhaven swore. "Damn it all to hell, you're right." Turning with a smile that was far from reaching his eyes, the duke offered hospitality to his unwelcome guests.

Lord Dunston eyed the duke intently. With a questioning glance at his son, he agreed.

Lady Windhaven stood, causing the gentlemen to follow suit. "Excellent! Dinner is at five, gentlemen. Now, Mrs. Benson will show you to your rooms. A rest is just what you need."

Hardly able to reject the dowager's orders, everyone filed out. As she passed by her grandson, she winked. Tristan wondered what was in the old woman's mind.

Raven stared, her mouth open. "Did she just wink at you?"

Tristan, no less astounded, nodded. "What the devil is she up to?" he wondered aloud.

"I like her," Adam told them, a huge grin suffusing his saturnine features.

As one, Raven and Tristan turned to stare at Adam as though he'd sprouted an extra head. He shrugged. "Well, I do."

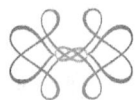

Tristan drew Raven into his study, firmly closing the door behind them. Pulling her over to the fire, he bent down to throw an extra log on the blaze. He turned to find her standing behind him, staring down in to the flames. He had the feeling she was lost somewhere in her mind.

"Rae, darling," he murmured, rising to take her hands. "What's going on in that pretty head of yours?"

She smiled. "That was Gerry, Tris. The boy from my memory. My best friend. Gerry."

"Gerry, eh? Your brother?"

"My twin, actually."

She met his eyes then, pulling her hands away. "You know, I always had this feeling I was being watched. It only added to my shame. I assumed it was God." She laughed lightly, trailing her hand along the back of a chair, her words and actions distracted. "All along, it was Gerry. It was the feeling of him. Hmm."

"Do you believe you are Rachael?"

Looking up, she brushed a hand over the chair back with a singularly graceful sweep. "Yes, Tristan. I believe I am."

Chapter Sixteen

It was with some trepidation and not a little nervousness that Raven emerged for dinner. Hence, she was every inch the Swan, serenely poised.

She had dressed in an evening dress of sapphire blue silk, cut in daringly simple but stunningly modest lines. It had the effect of drawing even more attention to her dark eyes and hair, which she'd had Meg pull up into a loose chignon.

As she moved down the hall, the supple gown swirled around her body. It did well to emphasize her curves, something Tristan couldn't help but appreciate. He stepped in front of her, gallantly offering his arm.

"May I escort you, my dear?"

"Thank you, kind sir."

Her smile had a whimsical quality to it that charmed him. Leaning close, he whispered, "You look ravishing, Rae, my heart. What say we skip dinner and adjourn to my bedchamber instead?"

"Oh, can we?"

He stopped dead in his tracks, the incredulity of his expression making her laugh. "Lord, Rae, I was funning. But," he added regretfully, "had I not decided we should wait until we are well and truly married, I would not hesitate to take you up on your offer." He grinned.

Raven frowned sadly. "Please do not bring that up again, my lord. My reasons for refusing you still stand."

Bowing, Tristan warned, "That may be, but know this: I don't give up easily." He stared hard at her, his eyes holding hers captive. "Or ever."

Dinner was rather pleasant, all things considered. Conversation was light and banal, focusing on the weather, fashion, or certain political affairs of interest to the titled gentlemen in particular.

Apologies were made for the absences of her grace's sister, Lady Gertrude, who was far too "ill" to be disturbed, and Lord Greyden, who was still in a rather insensible state due to his accident on the ice.

Raven sat at ease, none of her concern visible on her

face. Tristan's renewal of his suit had not really surprised her; his determination to triumph had managed to cause near panic.

She was placed beside Tristan—at his insistence—with the Earl of Huntley on her other side—at that gentleman's insistence, an arrangement with which she was quite content.

Unfortunately, the comte was beside Tristan's Aunt Hetty, who was directly across from Raven. Comte du Larousse had not taken his eyes off of her since they had sat down. And, cynically, she knew it wasn't her mind he found so entrancing.

A peal of delighted laughter, punctuated by several childish giggles reached them from the far end of the table. Adam, having been buttonholed by the Dowager to escort her in, was doing his humble best to entertain the old woman. Raven suspected he'd just told a less-than-proper anecdote, judging by the expression on the faces of those around them.

Raven sent him a severe frown, considering her young sister was seated beside him and couldn't have helped but hear his little jest. Adam merely shrugged, laughing at her.

Tristan drew her attention back to himself. "Rae, love, what has you looking so annoyed?"

"Adam is telling bawdy tales within my sister's hearing. She is only fifteen. She does not need to hear such things."

"She is not really your sister, you know," inserted

Gervase, Lord Huntley from her other side.

Raven started. This was not something that had actually occurred to her. Linnet was her sister in upbringing if not in blood.

Turning her head slightly, she met the earl's eyes. "Is Linnet someone I will be required to give up, my lord, should you decide I'm your missing sister?"

Her question was quiet, caught only by Tristan and Gervase. It was also blandly uttered, hinting at none of the latent anger buried underneath.

Except Tristan had come to know this woman rather well and sensed the incipient fury.

Gervase, for his part, frowned at her words. "Father would never dictate your choice of companions, Rae. Perhaps you could employ the girl as your maid."

She clenched her jaw, smiling thinly. "Indeed? Perhaps I could at that. I mean, what better life could she possibly have? The sister of an actress would not, after all, do very well in the marriage mart, would she? But as my maid, why, she'd have distinction…as the servant of an actress."

These words were spoken softly, gently, and with not an ounce of the rage Tristan knew she was feeling. He stared at Huntley, hoping against hope that the nodcock didn't say something to really set her off.

Gervase, more sensitive to Raven's moods than most of such relatively short acquaintance, sent her a look of admonition. "I was not suggesting you set the girl up for auction in a brothel or any such thing. You'd do well to hold your temper, sister."

Turning her head fully, Raven stared. "Excuse me?" she bit out. "Hold my temper?" She took a deep steadying breath, glanced at her brother again, and took another deep breath. Sending her love a look of patent disbelief, she repeated the calming exercise even though the excess of breathing was like to make her lightheaded rather than calm.

Feeling a good deal calmer, she returned her attention to her brother. "Linnet is my sister, Lord Huntley, and nothing more, nothing less. You'd do well to remember that."

Smiling, Gervase leaned close enough to whisper. "Bravo, dear sister. Never compromise. Take what you want and damn the consequences."

So saying, he turned and devoted his time to charming the lady on his other side—who happened to be Lady Montgomery.

Tristan was silently laughing. Taking her hand, he murmured, "I can't help but agree with him, my love. Why don't you follow your wise brother's advice?"

She scowled at him, pulling her hand away. "Leave it be, Tristan. You do not want to have this discussion here."

Lady Hetty, on Tristan's other side, inserted wisely—to her pug, "Oh, Horry, my pet, what do you think? The lovely earl is Rae's brother. He knows how to anger her and then cajole her out of it. Proof they are siblings. And the nasty comte is still staring. Think you Tris will beat him, Pugsy-poo? I should like to see that, I should..."—and as usual, she went off into some indecipherable language only the dog understood.

Tristan had to cover his smile with his hand. It was a rather uncomfortable statement considering the comte was seated next to Aunt Hetty and so heard every word the woman said. His handsome features flushed at the less-then-subtle insult.

Before the man could say something he would regret, Tristan intervened. "She is harmless, comte, an old lady who sees her pet as more human than people. Pay her no mind."

Aunt Hetty looked up from her pug long enough to send her nephew a piercing look, fully aware of what he was doing. Raven was startled to see such an expression of comprehension on the older lady's face.

The duke either didn't notice or chose to ignore it. Returning his attention back to Raven, he began talking of inconsequential matters.

The rest of the meal passed without incident.

Presently, the ladies adjourned to the drawing room, leaving the gentlemen to their port and cigars.

Raven entered the large room, moving with unhurried grace to the crackling blaze in the hearth. Stretching out her hands, she marveled that they were not shaking.

So many emotions roiled through her slender frame that

it was all she could do to keep it all trapped firmly beneath the surface. What she wanted to do was scream.

Sensing she was no longer alone, Raven turned to find the Marchioness of Preston by her side. Tensing inwardly for a rather ugly scene, Raven waited.

The titian-haired beauty raised one elegantly manicured hand. "Before you say anything, I want to apologize. It was unconscionable of my husband and I to assume the worst when we met you. It is clear that you love Tristan and would do whatever you have to, to ensure his happiness."

Raven's smile was strained. "I would," she admitted. "You know, then, that I refused his honest offer of marriage?" At Lady Preston's faintly guilty look, Raven scoffed lightly. "Ah, I see. Thank you for your thoughtful apology, my lady. Rest assured, Tristan's happiness is always foremost in my mind."

Satisfied, her ladyship moved away to sit and chat with Lady Montgomery.

A heartfelt sigh escaped Raven's lips.

"So sad, my dear. What has you looking so glum?"

Pasting a social smile firmly in place, Raven greeted the Dowager Duchess of Windhaven.

"I was merely thinking."

Eyes twinkling, the old woman placed an arm around Raven's waist, squeezing gently. "Ever a dangerous pastime, my dear. I do not recommend it."

The former actress laughed. "Indeed, my lady. I shall

endeavor to take your counsel to heart."

Frowning, Lady Windhaven replied, "I do wish you would not call me 'my lady.' Can you not bring yourself to call me Grandmother? Or perhaps Gloriana?" She paused. "My father was fond of calling me Glory," she confided.

"Oh but, my lady, I couldn't possibly. By now you have heard the circumstances under which I was invited here. Surely you cannot want the kind of relationship such informality suggests?"

"It makes no never mind to me, my girl, I assure you. It was very bad of you and that grandson of mine to try to pull the wool over our eyes as you did, but I am just pleased he has shown such determination to possess something he wants. He has been so lifeless since that useless son of mine died."

Startled, Raven admitted, "He said he wanted me to pretend to be his intended so he would be left in peace about marrying. It had nothing to do with me, personally, I assure you."

The duke's grandmother snorted. "Balderdash! Poppycock! That young man went to London five years ago and saw you as Juliet. He fell in love with you then. He returned thoughtful, preoccupied. It took some managing to discover the source of his preoccupation, let me tell you. When I discovered it was you, and who you really were, I encouraged him to marry, hoping he would be driven to extremes. And, low and behold, here you are."

"You are a manipulative old woman, are you not?" Raven murmured with a blank expression on her face.

Lady Windhaven chortled in delight. "That I am, girl, that I am. Have no fear; my interfering is over between you and my grandson. It is up to the two of you to work out whatever little misunderstanding has come between you." She paused, her eyes narrowing fractionally. "Which doesn't mean I'm not there to listen, should you need it."

Before the old woman could move away, Raven asked the one question they had been preying on her mind. "Would you actually countenance an alliance between us?"

After a second of intent study, the duchess replied, "What matter what I think, my girl? It is your life and Tristan's, not mine."

More confused than ever, Raven watched her return to Lady Hetty's side.

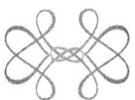

Tristan, as was his habit, declined the cigars and opted for an extra glass of the ruby-red port offered. He needed the liquid sustenance. His temper was already wearing thin and the ladies had only been gone a very few minutes.

The young Earl of Claremont, son and heir to the Marquis of Preston, had been allowed to stay, although not quite seventeen. His father had even allowed him port although he'd drawn the line at a cigar.

Tristan watched the young man, inwardly laughing at his

air of self-importance. Had young Deveraux known the kinds of mischief his father and Tristan had been into at that age, he would not think himself so privileged now.

It was with an unexpected pang that Tristan realized he could have a son on the threshold of manhood right now had things been different. He and Griff were of an age and, until the season Griff had met Delilah for the first time, they had done everything together.

Going off to war had changed much in himself and more in Griff.

Brushing aside such maudlin wanderings, Tristan returned to the present. He realized Huntley and Dunston were arguing in an undertone with the comte watching them, a small frown between his brows.

The words betrothed and comte were uttered, snapping Tristan's attention firmly on Gervase. Plastering a smile on his face even while his middle tensed with dread, the duke asked, "What's this, comte? Are you to enter parson's mousetrap?"

Dead silence filled the room. Even Will, good servant that he was, faded silently into the background, leaving the men in what seemed like privacy.

Comte Antoine smiled, a mocking look that Tristan immediately mistrusted. "We merely speak of Lady Rachael's betrothal to me. From infancy, I have known she would be mine. When she disappeared, naturally, plans were suspended. But now, should your actress"—the word was said with a certain amount of disgust—"prove to be Lady Rachael, the betrothal stands."

"That's interesting considering she is my wife."

The startled silence that followed informed Tristan that this salient fact had somehow missed them all. His own expression became mocking. "Gentlemen, I married the lady as Rachael Eliot. She is my wife, should you choose to acknowledge her as Lady Rachael. And should you not…" He shrugged. "It hardly matters then, does it?"

"But she cannot marry without her father's permission."

"Why not?" Tristan scoffed. "She is six-and-twenty at least, well beyond minor years."

Gervase, hitherto silent, inserted, "Rachael would actually be nine-and-twenty, Lord Windhaven."

Tristan's eyes widened. "Indeed?"

Dunston's laugh cracked across the now silent chamber. "Gel ages well, don't she?"

Adam smiled. "Perhaps you should keep her real age to yourself. I'm not sure she'll appreciate learning she's nearly three years older than she thought."

Tristan snorted. "I agree. Had you been able to tell her she was younger, maybe. But older?" He shook his head. "No woman wants to hear that."

A look of extreme annoyance crossed the comte's handsome features. Addressing Lord Dunston, he asked, "Why do you consistently speak of this woman as your daughter? As far as I can tell, she has given no proof that any actress worth her salt could not acquire. For me, I need to know positively."

"That is something we may not get, Antoine," said Gervase reasonably. "She may have nothing left that was hers before she disappeared. We will have to trust our instincts and mine say that she is my sister."

"She lost the locket you gave her," Tristan inserted nonchalantly, turning to the marquess. By the look on the older man's face, he'd been right to assume the locket had come from him and not from Emerson.

Gervase clutched at his waistcoat so suddenly that Tristan thought he might be having an apoplectic fit despite his age. He was relieved to see the earl was simply grabbing for a particular fob.

Lord Huntley tossed it towards the duke. "It was exactly like that, my lord. Except Rae wore hers on a chain around her neck."

Intrigued, Tristan scooped up the trinket. It was gold, intricately engraved. Releasing the little catch, he opened it to reveal two meticulously painted miniatures, a boy and a girl, identical smiles set in identical features.

And it was Raven in the right hand portrait. There was no doubt in his mind. Besides which, Gervase did look like the male version of her.

The duke narrowed his eyes at Comte Antoine. "Why are you so determined to believe she is not Lady Rachael? It would seem to be not in your best interest to claim she is an impostor."

"Ah, but as you so eloquently pointed out, my dear duke, should I accept her as Lady Rachael, I would lose my betrothed, as she is already married. I do not emerge the winner either way."

"Unless she is not a lady at all," Adam muttered, his pale eyes locked on the comte in such a way that Tristan was immediately suspicious.

In less than a second, Adam's meaning penetrated. But the baronet continued before he could say a word.

"What you seem to have forgotten, or misunderstood, or are just too stubborn to realize, Larousse, is that Rae belongs to Windhaven no matter who or what she is. She has made her decision and no one, not even Dunston, will change her mind on that head."

Tristan came out of his chair so fast, it clattered to the floor. "You bastard! You intended to convince Dunston Rae is not his daughter and then magnanimously set her up as your mistress?" Rounding the table, he went for the smaller man, grasping him by his shirtfront. "Had she decided to decline, what would you have done? Kidnapped her? Raped her?"

Shaking him like a rat, he snarled, "Whatever is decided, she is my wife, damn you! If you touch her, speak to her, hell, if you so much as look at her, I'll gut you like the animal you are!"

Tossing him aside, the debonair Duke of Windhaven

bellowed, "Benson!"

The butler appeared, Will at his side.

"Get this refuse out of my house!"

Benson snapped his fingers. Two more silent footmen appeared and between the four of them, they removed the insensible comte from the duke's explosive presence.

Tristan swore long and fluently. Rounding on the hapless marquess and his son, he snapped, "Did you know what he was when you brought him here?"

Gervase, calm as ever, replied, "We did not, your grace."

His father nodded his head in agreement, a flush of anger on his thin face. "Had we known, I'd have torn up that betrothal contract myself."

Somewhat relieved by these assurances, Tristan managed to calm his breathing. He wanted to go after the comte and beat him to a pulp for even daring to think what he had.

Then it hit him. He knew with vivid clarity exactly what Raven had been talking about.

Going suddenly pale, he slumped down into the nearest chair, which just so happened to be the comte's. Propping his elbows on the tabletop and dropping his head into his hands, he muttered, "She was right. Damn me, she was right."

Lord Preston, having known the duke the longest, was firmly urged to discover what ailed the man. Not by any means thankful for this duty, he nevertheless interposed, "I have rarely known a woman to be right about anything, my friend."

Tristan's head came up, his eyes hard. "What are you blathering about?"

Preston shrugged. "Women. Rarely ever right. They like to think otherwise, but…"

The duke laughed bitterly. "In this instance, my friend, I'm afraid you are very, very wrong. I will not go into details, but suffice it to say, Rae was wholly correct."

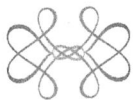

Chapter Seventeen

Family and friends gathered in the library the next afternoon.

Raven was as nervous as if she was about to set foot on stage for the very first time. And, in a way, she supposed she was. The only difference was, this would be the performance of her life.

Frighteningly, all she could do was tell the truth. What her audience did with that information was up to them.

When everyone had assembled and was seated comfortably, Raven stood. The gentlemen would have stood as well, but she firmly waved them back.

"Where shall I start?"

"The cat, the locket, and Gerry," Tristan suggested,

oddly reserved in his manner.

Raven smiled faintly. "Monsieur Boots was my orange tabby cat. Father gave him to me but wouldn't let me keep him."

Lord Dunston interrupted. "I gave you that blasted feline and a troublesome creature it was, too. Became uncontrollable after you…left."

Raven nodded. "As I suspected, it was Fath—Mr. Emerson who made me turn the cat loose."

Moving slightly away from the assembled company, she added, "I lost the locket. I don't remember anything about it other then it was gold and engraved. I assume it held a picture or two, but I…I can't remember."

"It looked like this," Lord Huntley inserted, holding up his fob.

Raven moved forward as if in a daze and reached for the bauble. "Ye-es," she said slowly. "It does look similar. But"—her brow furrowed—"the shape is different. Mine was oval. This is round." She released the catch. The twin portraits gazed up at her. She smiled. "I remember. We were amazed, Gerry, that someone had painted our portraits and we had never had even one sitting."

"Yes," Huntley whispered. "You suggested father had a spy lurking in the bushes, watching our every movement."

"Which wasn't far from the truth, by God," Lord Dunston said with a wink.

There was a pregnant pause. The duke, clearing his

throat, asked, "What is your earliest memory of the Emersons?"

Raven turned, staring into the fire as if for inspiration. "I suppose it would be when Fath—Mr. Emerson took Boots away from me. After that, I remember Moth—Mrs. Emerson having Paradise when I was five, in 1799. I loved that baby. But she died, as did Mother's previous five daughters. Less than a year later, Wren came along. She lived until she was four. Dove was born in 1802 and lived three years. Then Linnet was born and I was sure she would die too. But she was stronger than the rest."

Pausing, gathering her thoughts, she hummed lightly under her breath. It was a song she couldn't remember learning, had just always known. It gave her peace; it was her mantra.

She was startled into silence when two more voices joined in, right behind her, then a third.

Spinning, she immediately recognized Linnet as the third voice. That made sense. Raven had often sang it to the girl as a baby and even up through her middle years.

The other two were Dunston and Gervase, humming so softly, she could barely hear them.

"It was you," she whispered, locking eyes with the Marquess of Dunston. "I assumed it was Fa—Mr. Emerson who had taught me, but it was you." And it followed that Gervase would know it too.

"It is apparent to everyone here that you are my

daughter," the old man said gently.

"So where does that leave us?"

"It is up to you, my dear. If you want to accept us, we are more than willing to accept you. If you choose not to, however, you may return to whatever life pleases you."

Magnanimous indeed, she thought.

"If I choose to be recognized, what happens to Linnet?"

The girl chose to interpose her own suggestion. "I will live with Adam and Bri and learn to be a sleuth." Her face was lit with pleasurable anticipation. Adam groaned.

Dunston laughed. "The child has some ideas of her own, it would seem. But I shall not toss her on the street if that is your worry."

"You would make her a servant." It was not a question.

Gervase laughed. "My fault, father. I led her to believe that was what you would do." Turning to his sister, he said, "I was merely testing you out, sister. I never believed you would actually agree to turn the girl you believed to be your blood into little more than a bonded slave. Had you been the avaricious little adventuress at first suspected, you would have leapt at the chance to remove her as a responsibility."

Quirking one brow in imitation of Adam at his most skeptical, Raven said, "Thank you...I think."

Returning her penetrating stare to the marquess, she asked, "What of my past? Will you put it about that I never was the Ebony Swan? Or will you simply ignore those who talk and pretend it never happened?"

At that, the marquess hesitated. "Again, it would be for you to decide."

"To be honest," she told them all, "I'm rather proud of my career as an actress. There are certain…things…I've done in the course of my career of which I'm not particularly proud, but they are a part of my past. I wonder if the past can be left in the past. Or will it be trotted out upon occasion to remind me of how generous you are in accepting me back into the family fold?"

Her words were aimed like darts, and like darts, drew blood.

Lord Dunston flushed, whether in embarrassment or anger was anybody's guess. "I would not do so apurpose, I assure you."

Raven nodded, as if satisfied. Tristan watched her narrowly. She locked eyes with him and he knew what she was going to ask next.

"What of my marriage to Lord Windhaven? Would your recognition make it legal?"

"Yes."

Her eyes implored Tristan to understand. He felt his heartbeat slow to a stop, waiting for her next words.

Raven hated what she was about to do. She gazed around the room, meeting everyone's eyes, one by one.

Lady Windhaven gave her a smile and wink, encouraging her to accept, she knew.

Lady Preston and her husband wore twin expressions of disappointed sorrow, as though they knew she would accept and were already mourning Tristan's incipient misery. Their son seemed pensive, but he was not an easy person to read.

Freya scowled as usual; Linnet sat biting her lip, a sure sign she was thinking of something other than the proceedings. Adam was blank-faced, leaving the decision entirely up to her.

Lady Montgomery glared awfully, as she had since Raven had joined the household. Lady Hetty murmured to Horatio in an undertone, telling the animal only God knew what about them all.

And Tristan, ah, Tristan. The poor man sat with his face set in lines of displeasure, afraid of hoping, but knowing deep down what her response would be.

Turning back to the man she know knew was her father, and the man she knew was her brother, she said in a dead voice, "I am very sorry, my lords. I am not your daughter, nor your sister."

The duke thought he just might cry. His eyes filled with tears and it was only by an inhuman amount of will that he managed to keep them from slipping down his cheeks.

They had been given a chance and she had thrown it away for what basically amounted to her silly pride.

With a frustrated growl, he stood, intending to take his leave with as little grace as humanly possible.

At the last second, he stopped beside his love, staring up

at the ceiling. When he spoke, his voice was raw with emotion, defeated, saddened, and...lost.

"It always has to be your way, doesn't it, Rae?"

When she didn't respond, he glanced down at her. "Will you so easily forget what we were, what we are, to each other?" Moving fractionally closer, he whispered, "Will you forget this?"

He moved so quickly that she didn't know what to expect. With an arm around her waist, he pulled her flush against him. She was sure he would mark her somehow but...

It was the tenderest of kisses he placed on her lips. He drew back almost before she felt it. Opening eyes that had closed of their own accord, she stared up into misty green eyes, aching with love.

And her own eyes filled with tears. "I love you," she whispered. And determinedly pushed away from him.

Moving away, she turned her back on him and walked out the door.

And just like that, she was gone.

Chapter Eighteen

Good God, she'd only planned to go for a walk to clear her head!

Raven swore a blue streak at the figure in the driver's seat of the wagon. Unfortunately, he heard nothing more than a few angrily garbled words through a tight gag. And she could not see if he even registered her attempted insult as she was blindfolded as well.

She was trussed up like a Christmas goose in the bed, bumping and jouncing along, collecting only the Lord knew how many bruises, going only God knew where. What had she ever done to deserve this?

A groan escaped her as the wagon wheel hit a particularly deep rut and bounced back out. Just for good measure, Raven was slammed into the side of the conveyance, jamming her head and shoulder with excruciating force.

Her world went black.

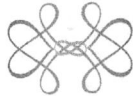

"Dammit, I told you not to hurt her!"

Raven inwardly winced at the painfully loud voice.

The statement was answered with what sounded like an uncaring grunt.

"Is she even alive?"

Raven struggled to make out something familiar in the tone and accent of the speaker. She gave up when the voice dropped to no more than a heated whisper.

A pounding commenced in her brain that was too painful to ignore. She released a groan much against her will.

"Ah, she is alive then. Wonderful."

Then she heard what sounded like a gunshot. The sound made her grit her teeth, wishing suddenly that she were dead. The reverberations ricocheted in her head long after the aftershocks died away.

Her gag and blindfold were removed.

"You can open your eyes, my beautiful bird."

"I'd rather not," she gritted out, her voice made unusually harsh and gravelly from lack of moisture and use.

"But, you see, I'd like you to. And what I want, I get."

The clear threat in the words belied the gentle, bantering tone of the user. Raven acknowledged that, for the moment, this madman was in control and she had best comply.

Besides, considering she could no longer hear the driver, she was quite sure he was the receiver of the recently fired bullet.

Taking great care, the actress slowly forced her eyelids up, blinking and squinting against the meager light of sunset.

She noted that she was cold but not freezing. She was wrapped in a heavy wool blanket. Her shoulder ached abominably and her neck felt like she'd been sleeping in a chair…for a week at least.

"Ah, there's my beautiful bird," the voice taunted, a caressing note in his words that Raven couldn't like.

Turning just enough to see her companion, she squinted against the fading sun. She couldn't make out his features as he stood with his back to the light.

But there was something in his voice that struck an odd note within her. It was a voice she'd heard recently…and yet it was one she hadn't for heard many years, as well. She just couldn't place it.

Forcing down the grimace that threatened to twist her features, she asked, "Would you mind terribly telling me just what the devil you're doing?"

"Watching you, my lovely, what else?"

Raven just blinked, her face blank. "Why have you

kidnapped me?"

He tsked. "Kidnapped? Such an ugly word. Spirited you away? Ah, yes, that's better. Has a nice romantic ring to it, does it not?"

She could hear the smile in his tone. She just wished she could picture his face. Where had she heard that voice and why did Windhaven jump suddenly to mind?

"But now, my dear beauty, we must adjourn to our little love nest. It grows chill and I must watch my health."

Raven couldn't stop the gasp of pain as she was abruptly lifted in strong arms, held against a broad chest. There was even something familiar in his scent, a little spicy but a little flowery, almost feminine.

It was only a few feet to the door of the cottage she had not noticed until now. It was small but neat, as if someone had recently been there to tidy up. She could see signs of wear and age in the peeling paint and faded rugs. The grounds, such as they were, had the look of neglect but only recently.

Where were they? They couldn't be far from Windhaven, as they'd only traveled that afternoon and into early evening. In fact, she wouldn't be altogether surprised to learn they were still on the duke's estate.

Upon entering the low-ceilinged, dim front room of the small building, her captor firmly kicked the door shut behind him. He set her on her feet and went to light a lamp.

There was very little light coming from the one tiny

window but Raven used what she'd been given to assess her situation.

There was a doorway straight across and a ladder going up to what appeared to a loft of some sort. The room in which they currently stood had a sort of kitchen in one corner, an open hearth with a large black pot suspended over it. On a small table next to it lay what appeared to be a cold repast of meats and cheeses, a bottle of wine next to the tray.

She suspected the other room was a bedchamber, the loft serving as a second one when the need arose. She doubted she'd be able to find any help for her situation in either of those rooms.

Turning her attention back to the kitchen, she searched with her eyes for a weapon of some sort, something to either immobilize or overpower her companion. She saw nothing but a small bread knife near the cheese. With an inward sigh, she realized it would have to do.

Finally having lit a merry blaze in the cold hearth as well as a branch of candles, her captor returned his attention to his unwilling guest. He was still in darkness, his features obscured.

"And now, lovely Swan, how shall we pass the time?"

Something in his voice finally penetrated her perplexity. He sounded like someone she'd recently met, minus a particular accent. Indeed, he sounded now suspiciously like...

He took a single step forward, a satanic grin twisting his handsome features. The light from the candles fell full on his face, highlighting pale eyes and pale hair.

As amazing as his appearance in this country was, Raven had somehow known who he was.

So, with something of an anticlimactic shock, she said, "How do you do, my lord? I was under the—obviously mistaken—impression you were dead."

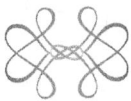

"She would not have simply left without word."

Adam hoped his tone and expression conveyed his confidence in this since he was actually unsure if he was even close to speaking the truth. Raven had become rather odd since meeting her duke. A woman in love and all that rot.

The Duke of Windhaven shrugged. "How can you be so sure? She was adamant about not accepting Dunston's offer. What prevented her from simply leaving?" *Surely not me*, he added silently.

"Her own sense of duty," retorted Adam, nearly fed-up with Windhaven's self-pity. "She would never have left Linnet. At least not without telling me or asking me to look after the child."

That was true. The little Tristan had seen Raven with her sister, she'd shown fondness and a certain air that was more maternal than sisterly. Which only made sense, as she'd raised the child.

"So, where did she go? She left yesterday afternoon and no one's seen her since."

"One of the groundsmen admitted seeing her walking towards the lake," Adam responded. "He said she looked 'all sad-like' and thought she may have been crying. He thought it was odd and watched her for a bit, but when she did nothing more than walk along the edge of the lake, he went about his business. He noticed later she was gone and assumed she'd returned to the house."

"What was she wearing? Surely she didn't leave the house in nothing but that flimsy gown she was wearing?"

"She wore her cloak. She would have been relatively warm for an hour at least."

Concentrating, the duke wandered over to the window without really realizing it. He stared out at the lake, cursing its existence in his life. As he stared, he went suddenly pale, and his lungs refused to draw breath.

Adam, noticing this, went to the other man's side, pushing him firmly into a chair. He moved away to the cabinet containing the duke's supply of brandy, poured out a hefty measure, and returned to shove it into the duke's trembling hand.

Feeling the slightest urge to slap Windhaven, he wondered the man if was having a fit. He was unnaturally pale and seemed not to know what to do with the glass he held. Adam caught the blasted thing just before the duke let it slip from his numb fingers.

Adam's cursing seemed to wake Tristan from the daze he'd fallen into. Noticing the glass for the first time, he lifted it to his lips, not caring what it contained. He quaffed the fiery liquid, relishing its burn.

Lifting haunted green eyes to the man who had inexplicably become his friend, he forced his horrified thoughts out into the open.

"The lake?" The words were no more than a broken whisper. "Could she have…fallen…fallen in?"

Adam, his eyes widening, went quickly to the window, wondering what Windhaven had seen to make him think such a thing. He stared at the thawing body of water, seeing nothing but an endless expanse of white, momentarily interrupted with dark spots where the water showed through cracks and holes in the ice.

His own face drained of color. He'd not considered the possibility of her falling in before. And now, he wondered why not.

Turning quickly for the door, he paused just long enough to drag Windhaven to his feet. "Come, man, we must search before it's too late."

The duke treated him to a funny look. "Before it's too late?" he repeated, almost mechanically. His expression turned distinctly pitying as he said, "Prestwich, had she fallen in yesterday, it is about fifteen hours too late."

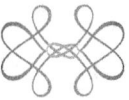

Despite the duke's very accurate assessment, a search was organized. Just in case.

Tristan was actually relieved. As much as he believed Raven had left because she couldn't bear to be with him, he took some solace in the fact that something was being done.

His momentary panic over the lake had faded to be replaced with the urgent feeling that she was still alive. He just wished he knew where.

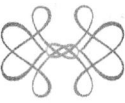

Two days after Raven's disappearance, Adam received a note from his friend, Lord Connor Northwicke, sent via Lady Brianna.

Bri included a note apologizing for the discrepancy between the date of the missive and the date she sent it on. It had become misplaced among some unimportant papers —namely society invitations.

Adam read the missive, cursed fluently in four different languages, struck the desk he sat at with his balled up fist, and flung the single sheet of vellum at his host.

Tristan, having watched this demonstration of displeasure with something akin to interest, took up the missive, scanning its contents quickly. His pale brows rose to reach his hairline.

"What has this to do with anything?"

"More than you could possibly know," snapped Adam from where he paced before the hearth. "Damn! Damn! Damn!"

Tristan ignored him, staring down at the note as if for inspiration.

The door to his study was suddenly thrown open with such force that it bounced off the wall. Both of the room's occupants looked towards the door, half expecting yet another calamity to have befallen them all.

It was Huntley, still in residence, and by the looks of it, thoroughly disturbed.

"He's taken her, I know!"

Tristan rose, pouring a glass of brandy. He carried it over to the distraught man, forcing it into his hand.

"Here, man. Drink up, calm down, and tell us what you are talking about."

It was several minutes before Lord Huntley was able to regulate his breathing, not to mention his temper. When he could speak, he told them what he suspected.

"Antoine, the bloody bastard. I don't know how father and I could have been so wrong about him. As a child he was rather quiet and reserved but very kind. He never would have hurt Rae, I'm sure of it."

Tristan shared a disbelieving look with the baronet. "Apparently, he has." As he uttered the words, a heavy sensation lodged in his chest, threatening to suffocate him.

The earl, having fully recovered his poise, looked up from his seat before the other two men. "Antoine would never do this," he insisted. His eyes dropped, a frown drawing together his black brows. "And yet he has."

"How sure are you that he really was Antoine?" the duke asked mysteriously, he and the baronet watching Huntley very closely.

A brief scratching on the door heralded the imminent appearance of Benson, distracting everyone from the duke's very pertinent, if rather odd, question. He bowed, offering the duke a card on a silver salver.

Tristan took it up. A wry smile crossed his grim features. "Well, what do you know?" He handed it to Sir Adam.

"Show him up," the duke commanded.

Minutes later the three gentlemen were joined by one more. He was shorter than the rest and startlingly fair, his pale blond hair worn rather longer than fashion dictated. He sported visible laugh lines and a rather careworn appearance around the eyes.

His face was unusually grim but he managed a strained smile for the company, gazing with meaning at the baronet.

Adam made the introductions. "Gentlemen, Lord Connor Northwicke."

Adam cut aside the usual inane greetings to ask, "What word?"

"Ah, so you did receive my note," Lord Connor murmured, glancing down at his drink. "In truth, not much.

He has been noted in London among other places."

"Who recognized him? Surely no one in Society?"

Connor shook his head, stared down in his drink for a long silent moment, then quaffed it. He wasn't much a one for drinking, but the stresses of the past few weeks had been hell.

"Derringer has had a small part since his return to England from God only knows where. In fact, he was the one who brought the news in the first place." He carefully set aside the glass, afraid he might do the unthinkable and smash it—or the unbearable and drop it.

Adam saw his friend's rather odd behavior and guessed rightly that the whole situation was wearing on him drastically.

"Con, leave it to us. We'll find him. In fact…"

Tristan stepped forward. "What kind of identity would he prefer to take on?"

Everyone stared at him. His face twisted in exasperation. "Would he, do you think, take on the guise of upper, lower, or middle class? Rich or poor? Titled or a just plain mister? Hell, would he masquerade as a servant?"

Lord Connor shook his head. "Never a servant," he said decisively. "Derringer mentioned a certain French aristocrat suddenly putting himself forward in Society. Actually, he claims Lord Dunston as his friend." He shifted deep blue eyes to the Earl of Huntley. "You are Dunston's heir, are you not?"

"I am," Huntley admitted without hesitation. "And if you are speaking of Comte du Larousse, I can say that yes, he is a friend, or was, rather."

"Was?"

Huntley nodded toward Tristan, suddenly overcome with anger, sadness, or a combination of both to the extent that he couldn't speak.

Tristan wondered if he would do much better. Clearing his throat, he said, "We suspect du Larousse has kidnapped Raven."

Lord Connor's gaze moved slowly from Adam to Tristan to Huntley. "You suspect he has taken Raven?" He turned to Huntley. "Do you not vouch for your friend?"

"No, my lord, I do not," the earl admitted. "Not anymore. He's changed. There's a ruthlessness in him I never noticed before."

Lord Connor paled with every word Huntley uttered. He stared past them all, into the leaping flames in the fireplace. Presently, he spoke.

"If du Larousse is actually my brother, heaven help Raven."

Huntley's expression was faintly perplexed. "Your brother, my lord?"

"The Marquess of Beverley," Adam supplied. "He's a little deranged and probably a little angry."

Lord Connor speared his friend with a look. "I was under the impression he'd been taken care of."

Adam shrugged. "He was dead the last time I saw him. But…"

"But…?"

"I didn't actually check his pulse, you know. He wasn't moving, he wasn't breathing; he fell overboard."

"You killed a man?"

Adam met Tristan's astonished countenance. "I have killed more men than I can count. And you, your grace?"

Tristan had nothing to say to that considering he'd been in the military and killed a few men himself.

Huntley was the one truly shocked by what he was hearing. Never having served in the military or been involved in anything remotely nefarious, he had yet to experience the necessity of protecting someone, possibly at the cost of a human life.

Tristan privately hoped the earl never had to undergo such hell.

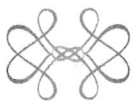

Chapter Nineteen

"So where do we go from here, Lord Beverley?"

Even Raven was inwardly surprised at the calmness of her tone. She was speaking to a man the world thought was dead—and good riddance—and she actually sounded as though she were inquiring about the weather.

He moved closer. His eyes gleamed in the candlelight, a manic flicker appearing now and then as he watched her, detecting her fear no matter how far down she buried it.

He methodically peeled off his gloves. Raven watched, mesmerized. His every movement was calculated, like a dance.

The man had a way about him, she had to admit. Even now, knowing what she knew about him, he was entrancing

"Come here to me, my angel," he cajoled, the hidden command unmistakable.

"'Said the spider to the fly,'" she quoted.

He chuckled lowly. "How I have missed you, my darling Swan. Have you missed me?"

"Like a toothache," she answered with complete, if not quite sensible, honesty.

He took another step closer. Raven determinedly held her ground although every instinct screamed at her to flee. She would not let this man see her fear.

For she did fear him. He was not right in his head. He made Lord Greyden, who had very nearly succeeded in his rape attempt, look like nothing more than a spoiled child.

It was a wonder that she had actually recognized him. He had changed a hundredfold since she'd seen him last. He no longer even remotely resembled the young, dashing marquess with the cruel streak and propensity for savage violence against women.

He was thinner, paler, and his eyes held a manic gleam that wasn't there before. His French accent when masquerading as du Larousse had been flawless. Had he not eschewed its use now, she might not have even realized they were one and the same.

"You do realize, of course, that by harming the daughter of a marquess, you will be hunted down and destroyed like the animal you are."

It was not a question.

And he laughed.

And Raven wondered if perhaps the devil himself had taken on human form.

In that instant, Raven knew there would be no escape for her. He would do what he wished; should she attack him, he'd kill her just as an insignificant insect.

But everything in her rebelled at giving in.

"I know well who you are, Lady Rachael. I've always known."

"Then you must know I am also the Duchess of Windhaven. The new king will not take kindly to his friend's wife being raped and murdered."

If possible, his smile grew. "My dear Swan, do you honestly believe I will be caught at this late date?"

Something of her fear must have shown on her face. His laugh this time was mocking—but he actually stopped stalking her.

"I will wait." His tone suggested she not view this as the reprieve it sounded. "Your fear will grow, heightening my pleasure." He grinned evilly.

But she honestly couldn't consider it anything but a relief.

He moved again, not stalking, but simply moved to her side gripping her arm painfully. He flung her across the room towards the back. She stumbled, catching herself against the opposite doorjamb.

"Sleep in there." With that, he walked out.

Raven's knees wobbled and gave out beneath her. She sank to the floor, as gracefully as she ever did as Juliet.

The sobs that threatened to wrack her body were determinedly held back. She had to think and she had no idea when he would return.

The Marquess of Beverley was alive. This seemed to echo through her panicked mind along with the thought that she would never get out alive.

Unless she killed him.

And she knew, without a doubt, that she would have to.

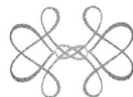

Blinking, Raven realized she must have fallen asleep. A sense of panic rose up to overwhelm her. Had he returned? Did she lose her only opportunity of escape?

It occurred to her that should she manage to escape, she had no idea where to go. She knew she was still near Windhaven but she had no idea in which direction they'd traveled.

Moving with incredible slowness due to the still aching sensation in her shoulder and head, Raven made her way back to the outer room.

Once there, she realized it was several hours later, full dark, and Beverley had yet to return.

She stifled the sigh of relief and strode over to the table. Grabbing up a hunk of cheese, she bit into it, determined to keep up her strength should the ability to flee arise. She could only manage to force a few bites before she tossed the rest back on the tray. The wine she avoided. He may have poisoned it.

Taking up the small knife, Raven tested the edge, pleased to see it was quite sharp. He must have believed she would not have the nerve to attack him—or else he didn't believe she could do much damage with the small blade. Regardless, she slipped the knife into the pocket of her cloak. Any sort of weapon was better than none at all.

She peeked out the door, meeting nothing but Stygian gloom in all directions. Light of some sort would have been nice, but she knew it would make her a sitting duck in the darkness.

There was nothing for it. She had to take her chances.

It didn't occur to her to wonder at the unbolted door.

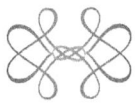

She had been walking for what felt like hours. She passed trees, denuded of their leaves, eerily grotesque in the dim light cast by a partial moon breaching the clouds.

The cold was starting to seep into her bones. Shivering, she pressed onward, sure she was going in the right direction and, even if she wasn't, the well-worn path suggested something was at the other end.

Then she heard it. The cracking of a twig or branch.

Glancing quickly to her right, she stopped moving, listening with all her might.

Utter silence.

Cautiously, she began to move again. Another twig snapped. She stopped.

Nothing.

Her heart pounding in her throat, Raven tried not to think of brigands, wild animals, and most of all, Lord Beverley. If she pondered what might become of her should she stumble across any of those three, she just might go stark, staring mad.

Closing her half-frozen fingers around the knife in her pocket, she began moving again, watching all around for signs of her unwelcome companion. She prayed that she could remember even half of the self-defense measures Adam had insisted on teaching her.

This time the sound came from her left. Were there two of them, who or whatever they were?

Turning slowly, she tried to pierce the inky darkness behind her. Still turning, she scanned all around her, looking for any sign of someone else.

Presently, she came back to her starting point, looked straight ahead…

And screamed.

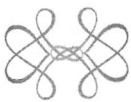

"My lovely bird, where do you think you are going?"

His tone held the same inflection one would use to comment on the weather, as though he had no real interest in her reply.

He probably didn't.

Raven gripped the knife tightly, almost tempted to move closer to him. His lips twisted sardonically, as if reading her thoughts.

She cautiously pulled the knife from her pocket. Beverley watched her movement, his smile growing until he released a short laugh.

"What do you hope to do with that, my pretty raven? Will you stick me between the ribs? Here, let me help." He opened his cloak and jacket, unbuttoned his waistcoat and shirt, exposing his chest. Pointing, he continued mockingly, "Right here, my dear Swan. Stick it here if you want to do me in."

Not pausing to think, Raven threw herself forward. She kept the knife up, hoping he would watch it.

He did. He never saw her other fist until it was too late.

Being a woman, her punch did not contain the power she might have wished but it was enough to knock him off balance. He stumbled to the side, surprise and then rage contorting his features.

Raven didn't hesitate then to strike out with the knife. She struck out and up, catching him exactly where he had pointed, between his ribs near his heart.

He fell back, falling slowly to the ground in what Raven personally thought of as a slightly overacted death scene. His eyes grew huge in his white face as he clutched frantically at his chest, rivulets of blood seeping through his fingers to drip and pool on the ground.

Raven stood transfixed. The coppery smell of spilled blood filled the cold night air, making her gag. She finally managed to stumble away to retch in the bushes.

Glancing back, she noted how still he was, his eyes open, unseeing.

She supposed, considering his propensity to come back from the dead, she should walk over to make sure that he was actually gone. After a moment of consideration, she decided she simply couldn't get that close to him.

So she skirted around him, continuing in the direction she had already been traveling.

Chapter Twenty

She was sure several more hours had passed. Streaks of dawn colored the night sky. By now, she was shaking uncontrollably, her feet and hands were numb along with parts of her face, and moving forward had become a matter of momentum rather than actual movement. It was only a matter of time before she would fall down, succumbing to the overwhelming urge she had to sleep…and never wake up.

But she was determined to go as far as possible. She would not die knowing she hadn't even tried.

If she actually made it, she swore she would do whatever Tristan wanted. If he wanted her to stay his wife despite the probable scandal, she would not decline the honor.

How she was able to walk away before was something she didn't understand now, and maybe never would.

Her preoccupation was shattered by the smell of smoke. Looking up, she realized she had stumbled across a small farmstead. Forcing her feet to turn in the direction of the building, she made it halfway down the short lane before she collapsed.

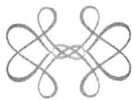

The search continued. Tristan sat at his desk, taking care of certain things that simply couldn't be put off any longer —as he had been ordered to do by Lord Connor after telling that gentleman to go to hell. He had been a little too anxious and had stopped paying attention to what he was saying. He knew Northwicke was hoping the normality of everyday life would help calm him. He had no such hope but diligently tried. And he hoped that by allowing Prestwich and Northwicke to take the lead, they would find Beverley. They knew him the best, after all.

Lord Huntley burst through the door.

"They found a body!"

Tristan's heart stopped. He had to swallow around a sudden lump in his throat. Please don't let it be Raven, he prayed silently.

"Who?"

The earl shrugged. "Some peasant, apparently. He'd

been shot through the head. They suspect it was Beverley."

Tristan released the breath he'd been unaware he'd been holding. "Indeed? Where?"

"A few miles west of here towards Speldhurst."

"Speldhurst? Has the area been thoroughly searched?"

Huntley nodded. "They found an abandoned cottage with evidence of recent habitation. Prestwich suspects it is where Beverley took her."

Tristan stared at him blankly. "So where are they?" he asked, meaning the marquess and his captive.

Huntley shook his head. "The search is continuing on to Speldhurst. Lord Connor suspects Raven may have escaped and tried to make her way there."

It was the first time the earl had called his sister by her adopted name. Tristan looked at him with sympathy, wondering if perhaps the younger man had finally decided to accept her decision to maintain her obscurity.

As if reading his mind, Huntley grimaced. "It's hard to think of her as Rachael when everyone calls her Raven, you know. Besides, no matter how much we all may wish it, she is no longer the pampered daughter of an aristocrat." He sighed. "She is Raven more than she ever was Rachael."

The duke commiserated with the earl. "I understand," he said softly. Then, with far more optimism than he actually felt, he added, "Join me for a ride into Speldhurst. Perhaps Grey's wife has heard something."

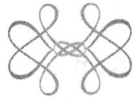

The two gentlemen caught up with the searchers just outside of Windhaven.

"What news?" the duke asked.

Lord Connor spoke up. "Nothing conclusive. There is some evidence of a tussle near Speldhurst but it could have been a couple of animals, for all we know."

The duke commanded his lungs to continue breathing. "Any blood?"

Adam nodded. "Quite a bit, actually. But, once again, it could have been a pair of animals."

"Very well. Huntley and I continue on to Speldhurst. Perhaps my brother's wife has heard something."

He ignored the twin looks of surprise on the other men's faces. Gesturing imperiously, he and Huntley left the others.

"Do you really believe Lady Greyden will know something, or do you seek to distract yourself?"

Tristan viewed his love's brother with a mixture of annoyance and amusement at his perspicacity. "Both, I suppose."

Huntley nodded, apparently satisfied. They rode on in silence, each watching for any sign of Beverley or Raven.

Huntley was the first to see the blood.

"Sir Adam did not exaggerate, did he?" the earl mumbled, looking a little green about the gills.

Adam had, in fact, underestimated the amount of blood spilled. Much of it had been trampled by several pairs of iron-shod hooves and blended into the dirt, leaving nothing more than a dark patch in the roadway.

Tristan swore, toyed with the idea of dismounting, then decided against it. "Let us move on. I'm sure this area has been well searched by now."

It was several hundred feet down the road that Huntley released an earsplitting scream. The duke turned his head in time to see the earl on the ground, struggling with what appeared to be a mass of tattered blankets.

Another scream erupted. Tristan realized the ragged mass was a man, apparently a madman. Cocking his pistol, Tristan tried to sight in Huntley's attacker but they moved too much.

With a grunt of annoyance, he dismounted and strode to the men on the ground.

It wasn't until he nearly stepped on them that he realized the ragged mass of humanity was the very man for whom they searched.

Growling with instant fury, Tristan reached down and hauled the man off the earl, shaking him until he ceased moving.

"Where is she?" he barked into the man's face.

Raising his head slowly, the man the duke was informed was the Marquess of Beverley—whom, incidentally, he'd met once several years ago—met his eyes with a look so demoniac that Tristan could not help himself. He recoiled.

Never, in all his years, in all his travels, battles, etc., had he ever encountered such an expression. This man was far beyond mad; he was possessed.

With morbid curiosity, the duke asked, "Did you sell your soul? Is that how you survived Prestwich?"

Beverley laughed, a low, eerie sound that sent shivers of unease skittering along Tristan's spine. Without really realizing it, he loosened his hold on the man, who used the opportunity to slip out of his grasp.

And the Duke of Windhaven, frightened beyond anything in his vast experience, didn't hesitate. He raised his pistol towards the fleeing man and fired.

The shot flew straight, shattering Beverley's skull. Blood and brain matter flew in all directions. The nearly headless body slowly collapsed, falling to the ground in a tattered heap.

Bile rose up in Tristan's throat at the sight. Despite the realization that he'd actually had no choice, he was sickened. He dropped to his knees, afraid he would disgrace himself by retching violently.

Glancing to the side, he realized the earl wasn't moving. Peering closely at him, he groaned.

The Earl of Huntley had been stabbed in the chest. Tristan very much feared he was dead.

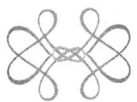

A furious knocking on the door startled Lady Greyden Cramshaw. She looked up from the book she'd been reading and glanced at the door. She knew one of her sisters would answer the door, but she pushed herself to her feet anyway, muttering a distracted excuse to her silent companion.

When she reached the outer hall, she encountered the man she knew as the Duke of Windhaven. Her jaw fell slack. He was carrying a man who appeared to be dead, struggling under the man's considerable weight.

Lily's sister, Violet, stood there, her mouth hanging open as well, obviously out of her element.

"Violet, show the gentlemen into the parlor. There is a sofa in there, your grace, where you may place him. I will have Daisy and Molly prepare rooms for you both." She moved to allow them to pass, her eyes modestly downcast.

The duke stopped briefly beside her. Speaking lowly, he said, "Thank you…sister." Her eyes flew up, shocked and a little perplexed. He smiled gently at her. "Things will be made right," he promised. So saying, he turned and followed Violet into the front parlor.

Lily was momentarily too stunned to move. Never in her life had she anticipated the knowledge that Greyden was actually related to the duke despite their surname being the same. Being accepted now by his family was an honor unlooked for. She'd never even really had her husband's acceptance. She was not naïve enough to believe the man had ever loved her.

Shaking her head against such thoughts, she moved to find her youngest sister and the maid, smiling in wonder as she went.

Tristan placed Raven's brother gently on the sofa, being careful not to jar him too much. The knife had penetrated so close to his heart that Tristan was unsure how the earl had managed to survive. But the short blade had just missed, having been inserted one rib too low.

Sinking slowly into a nearby chair, the duke dropped his head into his hands, wondering just what he was going to do. If the earl died, Tristan was quite sure Dunston would soon follow. The man had already lost a daughter, more or less, and to lose his son and heir would prove too much.

And Raven. How would he tell her, when he found her, that her twin brother had been killed? Even if she refused to accept the relationship, he knew she felt the bond that only twins share. It would kill her.

"If you'd like to remove him to a chamber, your grace, you may do so."

Tristan looked up at the softly spoken words, momentarily confused. Then his vision cleared. Grey's wife, Lily, stood just within the door, gazing at him with a directness that she hadn't shown before.

Glancing over at Huntley, Tristan sighed. "Perhaps we

should wait for the doctor. I dare not move him more than I have to."

Lily looked at the earl. "Perhaps you are right. It might have been best to take him directly to a bed. I'm sure it would be far more comfortable." She shrugged, her silvery eyes filled with compassion. "There is little we can do about that now."

She came further into the room to stand next to the injured man. "I can do a little for him until the doctor arrives, if you permit it, your grace."

"By all means, Lily, do what you can. I can help in some capacity, having some experience with tending wounds."

As if on cue, a maid—Molly, the duke assumed— entered with water and cloths for bandages. She set them down upon a little table near the sofa, bobbed a curtsy and inquired if there was anything else.

"Send Miss Violet in, please. Inform Daisy she is to stay with the children. That will be all."

Molly bobbed another curtsy, throwing an awed look at the duke, and left.

Lily sat gingerly beside the earl, her bent legs bearing most of her weight as she attempted not to jar the man. Hastening forward, the duke brought forth a low stool, setting it down beside the sofa.

"Here, sit here. If you fall you could do the child an injury."

Once again, her startled gaze met his. She glanced

quickly away, carefully removing the earl's bloodstained outer clothing.

"You know much about me, your grace," she murmured.

He shrugged nonchalantly, stooping to help her. "Not as much as I'd like," he admitted readily.

The earl's greatcoat and jacket fell away, to be presently joined by his waistcoat and cravat. The duke and Lily paused, staring at his shirt, plastered to his chest with an alarming amount of blood.

Lily swallowed hard. Tristan watched the working of her throat, wondering if she was going to be sick.

"If you'd like to leave, please do so," he offered, seeking to shield her from unnecessary distress.

Shaking her head firmly, if a little jerkily, she replied, "No, I am better. It is always the same when I see blood. I apologize, your grace."

Tristan reached forward and ripped the earl's shirt down the front, being careful only to avoid touching the wounded area.

"I wish you'd call me Tristan," he muttered as he worked. He heard the slight intake of breath from his exceedingly fair companion and spared her a glance.

"I couldn't do any such thing, your grace. You are far above me."

He snorted. He couldn't help it. "Poppycock," he said, using one of his grandmother's favorite expressions. "You are married to my brother. And to speak to or see you, one would never assume you were anything below gentry."

He peeled back the shirt fractionally, wincing when Huntley's body jerked spasmodically.

Lily, having soaked a cloth in the warm water, gently placed in near the drying blood. In moments it was loosened enough that they could fully remove the garment.

"How it appears is not the issue," she said then, returning to their previous conversation. "I am of low birth, no matter how much anyone tries to change me."

Releasing an exasperated sigh, the duke stopped cleaning the wound momentarily, fixing his sister-in-law with a stern glare. "Do you realize who I am, my lady?" he asked with uncommon arrogance, placing subtle but firm emphasis on her title. "I am the Duke of Windhaven. A bloody duke, pardon my language. If I accept you into the family fold, do you think anyone would dare to say the slightest thing derogatory about you?"

Lily gently took the cloth from him, cleaning the wound with painstaking gentleness. She said nothing until the wound was free of blood, revealing a rather savage gash beneath.

"It is not nearly so serious as it looked, I think," she said. "But it appears fairly deep. Stitches may be necessary. And it will probably scar." Suddenly turning her pale eyes to his, she asked, "Who is he, your grace?"

He blinked at her. "How remiss of me, Lily. This is Lord Huntley. He is Raven's twin brother."

"Ah, I wondered at the uncanny resemblance."

The earl jerked suddenly, causing a trickle of bright red blood to appear. Tristan quickly placed a cloth against it, pressing just enough to stanch the flow.

"She will be distressed to learn of this," Lily murmured, almost to herself.

"I wish I knew where she was to tell her," the duke found himself saying.

"B-but," Lily stammered, "she is here, your grace."

Blinking rapidly against the sudden blackness welling before his eyes, Tristan released the cloth he held. Lily rapidly snatched it up, pressing it back to the wound.

Tristan grabbed her other hand. "She is here?"

The duke crouched there for a full thirty seconds, unable to comprehend what he'd just heard.

"Yes, your grace."

"She's here?" he repeated stupidly. "Here?"

"She is here," the young woman reiterated with the utmost patience. "She stumbled into town yesterday morning. Mr. Brodie found her collapsed on his doorstep and brought her to me. He knew of our association and being a bachelor and an old man, he thought I could better care for her."

"Why did he not bring her to Windhaven?"

Lily's silver eyes grew liquid. "She would not have made it, your grace. She was nearly frozen as it was."

The duke sat back on his heels, stunned. "Nearly

frozen?"

Lily nodded. "She must have walked a great distance. Her hands and feet were like ice and she was liberally coated with blood. I have wondered what happened but felt she was too ill to be interrogated."

"Why did you not send for me, a message, something? I have been worried sick thinking she was dead."

Lily flushed at his admonitory tone. "I did not think it my place, your grace, and Raven—in one of her lucid moments—did request that you not be summoned."

Despite feeling as though he'd just been stabbed through the heart himself, Tristan surged to his feet. "Where is she?" he demanded, all the presumption of his station coming to the fore.

Molly entered then with Violet, the doctor following close behind.

"Violet, take his grace to Raven, please. Dr. Middlebrooke, Lord Huntley has been stabbed and needs stitches, I think."

Instead of taking umbrage at the young woman's assumption, the doctor peeked under the cloth and nodded his head in agreement.

"Quite right, quite right. Will you attend, my dear, or shall your sister?"

Tristan, not having left yet, inserted indignantly, "You cannot possibly expect her to assist you, doctor. She is in a delicate condition. It would prove far too taxing for her to assist in surgery."

Lily smiled slightly. "I assure you, your grace, it would not be too taxing, as I have actually done it before." She smiled at the doctor. "However, I think Violet's hands may prove a bit steadier this day." She waved her sister forward, who didn't hesitate.

Tristan watched, amazed as the girl washed her hands and prepared to do something, the very idea of which would cause most young ladies to faint. He couldn't help but admire these two young women.

"Come, your grace, and I will take you to Raven."

As they left, the doctor called out, "I will be up to see my other patient presently."

Lily led the way down the hall and up the stairs. Feeling a certain amount of urgency, the duke had to bite back the inclination to hurry her along, even though she was moving at a goodly pace.

Stopping before a door, she said, "I feel I should warn you, your grace. She is not yet coherent, most of the time and some damage was done by the cold. You may be a bit shocked by her appearance."

Dread filled Tristan's throat as he nodded. Lily opened the door, pushing it wide. She stepped aside, allowing him to enter first.

Lying amidst a plethora of white was Raven, the Ebony Swan. Tristan swallowed hard. She was awake, watching them enter the room, her dark eyes dull and lifeless.

"Oh, Rae," he breathed. His feet carried him across the room though he had little recollection of moving. He was beside the bed and reaching out for her hand, when he saw her flinch.

He jerked his hand away, perplexed. Looking at Lily, who had lingered in the doorway, he frowned.

"What did I do?"

An expression of innate sadness crossed the young woman's features. "She is in considerable pain, your grace. The damage from the cold was not too severe but once the numbness wore off the feeling in her extremities was restored, painfully so. To touch her will make it worse."

He nearly cried. He felt the tears pricking his eyes and felt utterly helpless. Dammit, he hated feeling helpless.

Lily sensed his need to be alone with Raven and mumbled an excuse to leave. He barely heard her.

Sinking into the chair that had recently been occupied by Lily, he sighed.

She looked so pale. Unnaturally pale. Her complexion was olive normally but now it closely resembled a corpse, paper white and translucent. Her nose and cheeks were an angry, swollen red and for a moment, he feared she was fevered. He quickly realized, however, that it was a result of the frostbite.

Her dull hair was drawn back from her face into a thick plait, devoid of its usual healthy shine and her eyes looked huge and dead in her face.

His gaze shifted to her hands, her beautiful, long, graceful hands. The tips of two fingers appeared almost black and he greatly feared she may lose them. The rest of her hand was white with angry red splotches where the cold had damaged her delicate skin.

"Be careful what you wish for."

Tristan started, once again meeting her eyes. Her throaty voice was a painful whisper, barely discernible over the beating of his own heart.

He shook his head, perplexed by her words. She laughed lowly—at least, he assumed the rusty croak was supposed to be a laugh.

"Once," she began haltingly, "said I would be ugly"— she swallowed—"preferred it."

He remembered. She had told him she'd much rather be loved for her mind and spirit than her face and form.

"Ah, Rae, my love," he whispered brokenly, "you could never be ugly."

Her lips quirked up into the semblance of a smile. "Gallant," she whispered.

"No, the truth." He drew in a ragged breath. "You have more good in you than I've ever seen." He left it at that, wisely understanding that at times, few words were best.

"Not good," she returned quietly but decisively. "Wicked."

"Nonsense," her love snorted. "You've seen wickedness, my love. Beverley was wicked. Do you believe yourself to be anything like he was?"

She closed her eyes, opening them almost immediately. "He is dead, then?" she inquired, ignoring the rest of Tristan's intense words. "I killed him?"

"No," he quickly denied. "I did."

Her smile told him clearly that she thought he was lying to protect her sensibilities.

He swiftly disabused her of that notion. "He attacked us on the road here. I shot him. He's dead. He can bother no one ever again."

"We?"

He hesitated, unsure whether she should know about Huntley or not. "Huntley and I," he said, evasively. "We were on our way to ask Lily if she'd heard anything of you."

Her expression clearly asked where her brother was. Tristan frowned.

"Huntley was injured. The doctor is with him now, stitching him up."

A tear escaped her eye. "Die?"

The duke firmly shook his head. "No, he will not die. The cut was small, but deep enough to require a few stitches. Given a few days of rest and little movement, he should be just fine."

"My fault."

"No, it's not," he snapped a little more forcefully than he'd intended. "It was a stupid, senseless accident perpetrated by a mad, senseless man."

"Sure he's dead?" she asked, moving her mouth as little as possible. "Comes back with frequent regularity."

He released a cynical laugh at that, knowing exactly to whom she was referring. "Trust me, my dear, Beverley is well and truly dead this time."

They lapsed into a silence that was not completely uncomfortable.

Finally, surprising them both, Tristan blurted, "Where do we go from here?"

She gave him a questioning look, remaining otherwise silent.

"I mean, do you ask me to leave and we forever part, or do I take you back to Windhaven as my wife, cherishing you for the rest of my days and hang the consequences?"

Raven just stared at him, her eyes suddenly bright. Her lips quivered, parted, then closed again. Her eyes fluttered shut and her hand clenched.

Reaching out, she grasped his hand, ignoring the obvious pain the action caused her. Then she opened her mouth and uttered the one word he'd honestly not expected to hear.

"Hang."

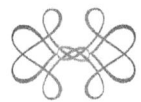

Epilogue

The Duke and Duchess of Windhaven were married again a few weeks later in a grand ceremony with most of the *ton* in attendance. It was apparent to all that it was a love match of epic proportions.

The main topic of discussion at the wedding, however, was the startlingly brilliant waistcoat sported by the groom. When asked about his choice of midnight birds on a pure white background, he and his wife would simply laugh, refusing to share the jest. Odder still was the blue-spotted lizards stitched on the border of the bride's satin gown. It was decided then and there that the Duke and Duchess of Windhaven were Originals.

It was something of a letdown, therefore, when the Marquess of Dunston announced that the duke's bride, the notorious Ebony Swan, was, in actuality, Dunston's long lost daughter, Lady Rachael.

An unprecedented amount of quite powerful peers—and most importantly, their wives—demonstrated their close friendship with the bride, effectively silencing the tongues of those foolish enough to say anything negative about her or her past career on the stage.

The sudden appearance of Lady Greyden Cramshaw was more climactic than anything that went before. She was quite obviously pregnant, and such a vision of ethereal loveliness that it was no wonder the young lord had done the unthinkable and actually married the girl despite her unremarkable parentage.

After two minutes spent in company with her, however, anyone who had any compassion—or sense—was completely won over by her gentle wit and innate sweetness. Lady Jersey was heard to say the girl was absolutely lovely, thereby securing her place in Society, should she choose to take it.

Lord Huntley recovered sufficiently from his wound, making an appearance at his sister's wedding. He was never seen far from Lady Greyden's side, a circumstance that caused much speculation considering the state of the lady's marriage to her invalid husband.

And Raven, finally having come to an understanding within herself, was able to ignore any stare that was less than respectful and any comment that was less than kind.

Her love for Tristan made her strong and his love for her made her invincible.

The End

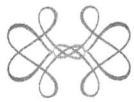

About the Author

Jaimey Grant, a pseudonym for Laura Miller, was born in Michigan in 1979. After a fun-filled childhood interlaced with moments of emotional trauma and an insatiable curiosity about the reasons people act the way they do, she became a writer.

Primarily a Regency romance author, Jaimey has also dabbled in fantasy of a non-romance variety. A comprehensive list of works and where to find them can be found on her website, www.jaimeygrant.com. There are more Regencies and fantasies in the works.

She currently lives in Michigan with her husband and two children.

To learn more about Jaimey and her work, visit any of the sites below.

Website: http://www.jaimeygrant.com
Facebook: http://www.facebook.com/jaimeygrantauthor
Email: jaimeygrant@yahoo.com